The Prairie Drifter

Volume 2
The Long Road Home

A novel by

Richard Wyn Jones

To my Mother and her love of the Wild West

By the same author:

A SQUIRREL'S TALE

THE PRAIRIE DRIFTER - Vol 1 - *Journey of Discovery*

CONTENTS

The Prophecy

When the Prairie's bled and broken
Crying out for all to see
A changeling child will be awoken
Born to set the Mustang free.

His fate, to find his lifelong purpose
Suffering shall be his way
Understanding words strange spoken
Chased by evil all his day

The elements of nature's ire
All will soothe his bitter pain
'til the world can bring desire
To restore their place again

Sacrifice shall be his meaning
Healing all the sickened herd
Of all secrets will his learning
Bring back balance to their world

When he understands his calling
Then the skies will darken so
All the animals that seek to harm him
Will unite to smite his foe

Only when this veil is lifted
Will his spirit then be free
Arion will come to take him
To the heavens eternally

Prologue

Since the death of Abrazo and the overthrowing of Zell, Shade continued to consolidate his power over the Prairie herds. His fanatical Zellats ruthlessly carried out his will and oppressed those who opposed him.

Hope faded, but a few still believed.

Halden, the old storyteller had predicted that Star, Abrazo's son, would have a part to play in an ancient prophecy and although his birth was concealed from Shade, suspicion was later aroused, and the young colt was forced to flee for his life, along with a small band of friends.

Star, became separated from his companions, presumed dead, following a buffalo stampede, but he was found and nurtured slowly back to health by Flying Hawk, son of Chief Brown Elk.

Migisi, the Eagle, refused to believe that Star was dead, searching the country for her friend, eventually finding him at the native camp.

Hounded by the bluecoat soldiers, Flying Hawk's father made the painful decision to take his starving people to live on the Reservation. The heartbroken young brave set the young Mustang free believing that where they were going was no place for a wild horse.

Hesitant at first, Star was eventually convinced by Migisi that the only way to save his kind was to continue on his quest, and so the young stallion set off once again.

He would go north, in search of the White Bear and hopefully find his destiny.

Chapter 1

Star didn't stop running until he had left Flying Hawk and Migisi far behind him. It was a glorious feeling to be free once more. He breathed in the delicious smells and marvelled at the wonders of nature. He listened to the voice of the wind and stopped to look at every bird that darted by, or to examine every animal track around him. For a time, he just revelled in the wonder of running where he willed…Free.

After a while, that sense of loneliness returned, and his heart filled with sadness. Thoughts of his friends, his mother, the strange Prophecy, invaded his emptiness. The young stallion's mood began to change. He missed the companionship of the eagle and even began to realise how much he yearned for the company of the boy. He wondered what on earth this great, wise, white bear could tell him about his future and felt angry and confused every time he thought of the Prophecy. "Why me? Surely there is someone more worthy to carry this mantle?" Star snorted and shook his head. He galloped away as if hoping his speed would somehow leave all this behind, but again and again, the pain of responsibility came back to torture his soul.

Star was heading north now across the great lands. The first part of his journey had gone well. He managed to avoid contact with the humans. Here and there he saw evidence of their tracks and twice he saw their camp fires and wagon trains.

Eventually, he turned away from these trails. Solitude gave him the chance to reflect, and his dreams of returning home paled and seemed less attainable now. For several days, he hesitated about continuing, and he might have lingered longer still had not the weather turned milder.

The time of the growing grass moon was approaching, and with the longer days, his spirit began to lift, and a renewed hope filled his heart. The sun shone brightly in the middle of the day and for a while, extinguished the gloom.

In that time of uncertainty, after the snows about him had melted, the last traces of a young horse left him and if a weary sorrow for what he was leaving behind sometimes came to his eyes, so did a look of determination.

Instinct led him on, and with the changing season, he thought that somehow Arion was helping him. He had been a survivor for so long that the dry Plains across which he travelled seemed no particular hardship. When times got hard, and good food was scarce, Star had no trouble retreating into his dreams and memories where he found comfort and courage.

Unfortunately, the milder weather was not to last, and nature once more provided him with his sternest challenge. As the stallion journeyed further north, the Prairie winds grew colder. Star often spoke to Arion, which helped keep his faith in the mission.

"Arion, watch over me and give me the strength to fulfil my purpose. Let me not forget my destiny."

This time alone also helped clear his confusion, and his body became stronger for the suffering he had known. He hoped that somewhere, someone would hear his message, for isolation is a dreadful thing and loneliness a blizzard in a horse's heart that robs them of strength, his mind of purpose, and his eyes of hope. The young horse looked to the sky.

"Give me courage to continue this journey. Guide me…"

Gazing to the shining jewels on a clear, chilly evening and then to the distant silhouetted horizon, "to there I will go," he neighed out loud, a renewed enthusiasm and defiance in his voice.

His wandering mind began to imagine himself as the last of his kind. Like something that floated in the air, on a wind none could see which blew from place to place. A dry leaf, perhaps, or a feather from a young eagle's belly, a snowflake that floated against the run of all his companions, or the shine of a piece of dust, caught drifting for a time across the shaft of sun through a wooded glade. These things the stallion found himself to be. As he stared at the stars, he was there amongst them, far from the place upon which he lay. If he felt the earth, his body was its mountain ranges, and his limbs were its river valleys.

A great peace came to him, one from a deeper understanding for maybe what the Prophecy now expected of him.

The next day, Star stood poised near a wooded river. He had been following a trail which had led him along the bank and then disappeared where trees had fallen across the path of the water. Mud and branches were stuck together along the length of the timber, and the structure was roughly three to four horses in length and about the height of a stallion. Star viewed the construction with a puzzled intrigue. It was not human in origin but was quite magnificent in its scale. Behind the stream the water had formed into a large pond, flooding out to some of the surrounding low ground creating a wetland area.

He was about to turn away when he suddenly saw something flash over the surface. 'A fish?' he thought, but the trail it left behind suggested that it would have to be a big fish indeed.

Star paused, then he heard a dripping sound, and suddenly a dark shape slipped from the river and bustled across to a nearby tree and started to gnaw at the bark.

The young horse watched, blinking in disbelief, transfixed by this strange creature scurrying about on his short stubby legs, furiously digging up mud and stones with his sharp front claws, carrying them back and forth to the river. It was quite stocky in build, about the size of a small fox and covered with a coarse brown fur.

Understanding that there was no threat to him, Star decided to introduce himself.

"Hello," muttered the stallion.

The startled animal scampered to the safety of the pond, disappearing into the water with hardly a sound.

Star stepped forward.

"Hey there, come back!"

Star waited in anticipation, then suddenly its small head popped straight out of the water.

"Were you talking to me?" he asked.

"Yes," answered Star.

"How?" said the startled animal, showing his long sharp front teeth.

"I've always been able to do that."

The creature disappeared again and then re-emerged near the edge of the bank, shaking himself in a great spray of droplets as he clambered onto firm ground.

He approached cautiously, before sitting back on his large webbed hind feet with his paddle-shaped tail between them.

He studied the horse with a curious intent.

"Interesting…" he twittered.

"I'm a horse," said Star. "What are you?"

"Yes, I know what you are," replied the irritated creature. "My name is Kobet; I'm a beaver. What do you want?"

"I just wanted to say hello, that's all. It's been so long since I've spoken to anyone. My name's Star."

"Well hello. Now I can't stand around talking to you, I have so much to do, and my mate is sick."

"Sick?" said Star stepping closer. "What's wrong?"

"I don't know," answered Kobet sadly, "but she won't eat."

"Is there anything I can do?" said Star with concern.

"What could you do?" answered the beaver disdainfully. "You may be able to speak my language, but what do you know about beavers, eh?"

"Nothing I suppose," agreed Star, "but when we were sick, my mother used to find berries, bark and a particular type of grass that would make us well again."

"Yes. Yes, of course," said the beaver, "I know just what she needs, but this type of grass grows only by the sea, and my mate is too ill for me to leave her. Oh, what will I do?"

"The sea?" said Star, hardly believing his luck. "That's where I'm going. North to the sea. What is the sea exactly?"

"You've never seen the sea?"

Star shook his head.

"The sea is where the rivers go. The sea is the greatest water in the world. Magnificent it is. Went there just to look once. Curiosity. Wouldn't like to live there, though, water tastes strange." Kobet scrunched up his face at the thought of the salty taste before gazing once more at the stallion.

"Have you really never seen the sea?"

"No. I'm from the Prairies."

"Well, this is strange. First I meet a horse that can talk to me, then I find out that you've never seen the sea."

"I'll go for you if you like," said Star. "To the sea, I mean. I'm going that way anyway. I'll get your mate the grass you need."

"You?" exclaimed the startled beaver.

"If you'll give me proper directions."

Kobet eyed the horse carefully. "You mean it?"

"Just tell me where to go."

The beaver's face lit up enthusiastically. "Just follow this trail for around three suns, and the land will change," as he pointed his paw in a particular direction. "It will become flatter with few trees which slope gently towards the sea. Then just keep going."

Star nodded, and he set off promising to be as quick as he could.

"Thank you," chirked the beaver, as he watched him go. "I'll be waiting for you and forever in your debt."

Chapter 2

Just like the beaver had told him, it took three suns to reach a point where the trees began to thin out. Behind him now, were the lush forests of white spruce, balsam fir, aspen and white birch. Ahead, just a scattering of black spruce and tamarack spread over a vast sodden gently sloping plain of tundra browns and sedge meadow greens; a guileless and bleak landscape where only the hardiest of creatures could survive.

By the following sun, Star had scented something on the wind. It came to his nostrils, strange and bitter. Over the next incline, the land fell away. The stallion stood in wonder, for across the horizon was a vast sweep of water that seemed to stretch to eternity.

The biting cold wind tore and shook its turquoise surface into curls of foam.

"So this is the sea," he said to himself as he gazed at the distant moving water.

Despite the time of the year, strange imposing cliffs of white floated gently across the briny waves. Star looked on in awe at their creviced walls patterned with geometric shadows and a white that could make even the brightest of sun rays look greyed. It was, without a doubt, the most natural and perfect thing he had ever seen. It seemed incredible to him that something so large could simply float in the sea, no more anchored than a twig. They moved gracefully on the currents at such a gentle pace as to appear quite static.

"Now to find the white bear," he muttered to himself. Star realised that in the vastness before him, this might not be as easy a task as he had first thought.

High in the sky, a circling eagle had spotted her friend. She had flown north to make sure the stallion was safe. The great bird let out a loud screech which pierced the stillness around. Star lifted his head to the heavens, his mood energised immediately.

"Migisi!" he called excitedly, leaping about, "Migisi!" came the second call more with a tone of relief than anything.

The eagle came to land near the young horse. Star trotted across to greet her. He could hardly contain his emotions.

"I'm so glad to see you," neighed the relieved horse. "It has been so lonely these past weeks."

Star calmed, looking at his friend quizzically. "I wasn't expecting to see you. Nothing wrong?"

"Well, it occurred to me some weeks after you left, that you wouldn't know which white bear to approach, so I thought it best I come, just in case," replied Migisi.

Star's mood changed instantly. "You mean there's more than one?" muttered the now nervous horse, glancing around furtively. "And what do you mean, just in case?"

"Yes, there's quite a few of them, but they're spread out everywhere. Fierce lot they are too, much worse than your typical bear where you come from. Wouldn't do the Prophecy any good if you became their main meal would it?"

Star shook his head, a little skittish.

"Come on, follow me, and I will lead you to him. He's the oldest in the north. That's why he's the wisest. Be careful, though, he can also be a little grumpy at times."

"Does this bear have a name?" asked Star.

"Yes, but he likes to introduce himself. If you get that far, you've made a good impression." Then the eagle took flight.

"Wait! What do you mean if I get that far?"

But Migisi was already well out of earshot.

Star bowed his head to one side to deflect the biting onshore breeze keeping one eye on his friend as he plotted a cautious path forward and another on the increasing possibility of an encounter with an angry bear.

The bleak grey clouds overhead reflected his mood. The land lay barren and lifeless before him as if Arion himself had put it to sleep. As each footfall broke the frosted puddles that lay embedded in the hardened earth, the dampness crept into his tired limbs and made them ache for his home again.

Migisi was never far away and provided the necessary encouragement to his friend, in the final leg of his journey.

Then he came down a slope and Star felt the ground turn from sodden earth to a strange, soft powder that his hoof sank into as he walked.

Migisi circled overhead, screeching on the ragged wind, riding the currents of air. Star approached the edge of the water gingerly and marvelled at the frothing waves. The scent that had hit him so powerfully before came again, and he could taste it on his lips. He turned in a direction along the beach to follow his navigator.

Many times the young horse had seen the wind work on rivers and lakes, where it sprayed and flurried, but this mighty sea seemed to move as one, shrugging its shoulders against the land.

Star traversed along the shoreline, always keeping Migisi in sight. Just beneath the tideline in the distance, he saw an expanse of low-lying rocks blanketed with rows of pungent kelp. They had thick and rubbery stalks like stems of giant mushrooms that rolled and settled to the soothing ebb and flow of the incoming waves. Where it had been thrown high on the sand, where the water could not reach it, it had dried and crackled underfoot. The stallion sniffed it, and it smelt like the wind.

He nibbled at it, and it tasted bitter, but not altogether unpleasant. He sensed that there was something strong and wholesome in it and was sure that this was what Kobet had referred to.

Migisi landed on the soft sand next to the horse. "He is over there," said the eagle, gesturing with his beak.

"Are you sure it's him?" said Star.

"Of course, I'm sure. I'm an eagle. Now I really must be off. I've something important I must do."

"But you can't just leave," blurted Star.

"Take care and don't forget, be careful. Give my regards." Migisi took to the air and with one sweep of her wings, was a mere dot in the sky.

"Wait!" cried Star. Too late. He was alone again.

Fear gripped the stallion as the hint of another smell came subtly to him on the wafting breeze. The sinews in his body stiffened and alerted his senses to a threat.

Further along the seaweed bed near the shoreline, a large white form not unlike the shape of a small iceberg was stretched out motionless, save the gentle up and down movement of its rhythmic breathing. Next to this massive form, the rib caged remains of an animal was being picked over by a group of squabbling gulls.

Star's heart skipped a beat. His eyes widened in expectation. "He's huge," he gasped.

This was Star's first encounter with a bear of any description, and although he had been told by his mother how dangerous they were, nothing could have prepared him for this.

The anxious stallion approached with extreme caution and the closer he got, the more the size and scale of the creature almost took his breath away. A thick coat of white fur covered the gigantic frame, and a sleepy yawn revealed his cavernous mouth of razor-sharp daggers. The murderous capability of this fearsome brute was further evident by the red-stained white fur around his jaws.

Without warning, the polar bear sprung to life, his amber eyes flashed angry and menacing towards the horse. Star leapt back, scrabbling for a foothold in the wet slippery seaweed. The bear raised himself on his hind paws and let out a guttural roar that seemed to shake the world around him.

He dropped to the floor, his four huge paws anchored to the ground.

"Who is fool enough to disturb my sleep?" growled the angry bear.

Star wanted to answer but fear dried up the words in his mouth. Then in a shrieking blurt the horse cried.

"Migisi sent me!"

The advancing bear stopped in his tracks, his eyes narrowed.

"Migisi?"

"Yes," replied Star, backing off.

The bear stiffened his pose eyeing the horse suspiciously.

"How do you know Migisi?"

"I saved her once, from a man trap."

The beast considered the reply a moment and then began to pace back and forth.

"And Migisi said to come to me? Why?"

The nervous horse nodded his head. "She said you could help me."

He looked the stallion up and down. He paced some more, then halted. "I probably won't eat you just yet then, at least until I've heard your story."

The bear flicked out a single claw and began to pick at something lodged in his teeth before adjusting himself into a less threatening, comfortable position. The bear stilled himself.

"Begin then. And it better be good, for your sake."

"My name is Star. I'm from the lowland Prairies."

Star began to tell the white bear everything he knew. His home, of Kara the Mountain Lion, who told him of his cause, the Prophecy, fleeing from Shade and Zell, the Zellats and their pursuit of their group. The bridge, Goran the wolf and his meeting with Migisi. The loss of Muneca and how they met the strange ranch horses, his stay with Leonardo's herd and the buffalo stampede. But it was only when Star got to the part about man that the bear opened his eyes in amazement.

"So, you've spent time with humans?" he said inquisitively.

"Yes." Star nodded.

"Were you frightened of them?"

"Yes and no," answered Star. "There were times when I felt a strange power there, a kind of…" Star paused. "Well, a kind of violence. But at other times, with the youngling at least, I felt I almost understood him. Not so much his words, but what he was thinking."

The bear was quiet for a moment, as he pondered.

Star continued, "Migisi said you'd be able to tell me if there was any truth in the Prophecy and if it's better for my friends if I never return to them at all."

"What does your heart say?" responded the bear.

"I'm not sure, but the dreams, being able to talk to other animals… I don't know! Why me?" Star was surprised by himself. He had never before tried to convince anyone that there was anything special about him.

At this, the bear looked carefully at Star. "Mmmm… I agree, that is different, but does it prove there is a Prophecy, I don't know."

"What do you mean?"

"Well… How do you think I have a knowledge of the world? I've had a conversation with whales that would make your mane stand up on end. I've talked to albatrosses, though I wouldn't recommend it. They've got little to say for themselves. I've spoken with all manner of animals large and small."

"But I never learnt how to do it. Just happened," replied Star.

"You don't need to learn it. There was a time when all creatures could converse with one another. But somewhere in their self-thinking and fear, they forgot. Animals need to start listening again."

The bear's tone had grown rather severe.

"Long ago, it was different. Animals just seem to have lost the knack. Don't ask me why. The sea creatures can still do it, but that's the trouble with land, I suppose. It cuts you off."

Star looked rather relieved.

"But what about the boy?"

"Ah, no animal can talk to man and no animal should."

"But man is an animal too, isn't he?"

The bear paused. He looked at a loss.

"I suppose so," he said at last, "though even my knowledge of the world grows dark when it comes to man."

Star was disappointed.

"Oh, I know that man is always fighting, always killing. Even our kind suffers at their hands. I fear for our world if man rules. Much death will come to our lands, for man is the bringer of violence."

But as Star listened he thought of the boy again, and the little girl and how sometimes their eyes seemed so kind, but this merely served to confuse him more.

The bear looked at the perplexed face of the stallion. "Well I suppose, seeing as I won't be eating you then, I'd better introduce myself properly. My name is Nanuq."

For three suns, Star stayed with Nanuq, and the white bear told him everything he knew of the world. He spoke of healing ways, something the stallion took a particular interest in and when he asked Nanuq if he'd learnt this from his mother, the bear explained that some he had, but other things he had found out for himself. The secret, he said, was to trust in yourself and listen, for animals seem to have forgotten this value. Nature's scent and colour can also tell you so much about a plant's mystery and healing ways. As Star listened, the sea lapped and swayed as it had done since the forming of the world.

Nanuq also told him about what he knew of the Mustangs and what had become of his kind while Star had been away, He had heard that Zell was dead, murdered by traitors and that Shade now called himself Lord of the Prairie Bands and his Zellats were moving everywhere. There were some, a few Bands, to the north, that had resisted Shade's power. At this point, Star looked up with keen interest.

"My friends," he said, "do you have any news of my friends and my mother?"

"I'm not certain," answered Nanuq, "but the first night you stayed, I asked a gull to fly south to find more news."

"And...?"

"And he met Migisi, and she told him that while you were with the boy, something strange happened. The mares and your friends were driven south by a group of stallions and seemed to be travelling against their will."

"Why didn't Migisi tell me this herself when she led me here?" said Star.

The bear shrugged his shoulders.

"Migisi followed them, and when they had travelled a long way, they were met by another group and handed over."

Star detected hesitancy in Nanuq's voice.

"What is it?" pressed Star.

"Migisi recognised the leader of that second group..." Nanuq fixed his stare on the stallion.

Star's eyes sprung open in desperate recognition. "Shade!"

Nanuq nodded confirmation of this fact.

"But that means that my mother and friends are in Shade's clutches. He will harm them for sure. I've got to help them, Nanuq."

The stallion paced about, agitated and stressed.

"He means you more harm if he finds you are still alive. This is why Migisi probably felt it best not to tell you. Do try to think, young stallion," said Nanuq, almost angrily.

"You go charging in on your own. What will that achieve? How will that help? You are one, he has hundreds at least, behind him. Wherever you go he will be looking for you, his spies are everywhere, and they will kill you at the first opportunity."

"But my mother, my friends," said Star desperately. He pondered for a while. "I shall go back to Leonardo's Band, they will help me."

"Leonardo is dead, and they have submitted to Shade. Morro now rules there, and Migisi says he has an alliance with Shade."

Star fell silent. Though he felt a biting guilt towards his mother and his friends, mixed with a mounting loneliness, he knew that the white bear was right. That night Star hardly spoke, gazing for hours across the bitter sea.

The stallion woke the following morning after a fitful sleep. Nanuq was sitting nearby. He noticed the horse stirring.

"Ah, good you're awake," said Nanuq enthusiastically. "I've been speaking with others about you, and I think I have an answer to what you should do next on your quest?"

"My quest?" queried Star.

"To find out if this Prophecy has any meaning and whether you are indeed The One."

"But I thought you would be able to tell me this."

"I might have a knowledge of many things, young stallion, but this needs others who will be able to prove beyond doubt."

"Others?"

"Yes, to the west. They are horses like you."

"Why didn't you tell me sooner?"

"I had to be convinced that there was something in your story. They are a strange lot, so I understand, never really had much dealings with them. They live in isolation beyond the western mountains. Some say they are descendants from the original horses that crossed the great land bridge, thousands of years ago from the frozen lands beyond, and that they are direct descendants from Arion himself and the guardians of his spirit and the ancient ways. It is said they worship according to the old Lore and even have an understanding of Man. They have survived the harshest of climates, more than any other horse can survive. Some say they have special powers and that they are waiting and have been for hundreds of years, for The One, who will eventually deliver the Prophecy."

"So you think I should go there?" said Star rather disconsolately.

"If you want to find out."

"But what about my mother and my friends?"

Nanuq looked at Star, and he felt bitterly sorry for the stallion.

"You must decide in your own heart if you truly believe this Prophecy is real. But ultimately, whatever you choose, you must be very careful. Shade will do everything he can to destroy you."

"It seems that I am a danger to everyone now, whatever I do," sighed the thoughtful Star.

"Whatever, young horse, I fear that the outcome will not only affect the lives of your kind but of all creatures. Something is happening to the balance of our world. I am afraid a great storm will sweep us all away if we cannot change things for the better."

"Then I will go west. At least then I will find out what I am."

The bear placed a reassuring paw on the back of the stallion, recognising the pressure and responsibility that Star shouldered for all.

"So where should I go, Nanuq?"

"I don't know their precise location, but if you seek out a herd of female horses, the Maidens of Arion, that will be a good start."

The stallion looked intently at the bear.

Nanuq continued. "They live somewhere on the far side of the mountains and serve the Guardians. They collect berries and fungi, and now and then some stallions come and take away their young males. To find the Guardians, you will need to follow them."

"What do they want the newborn colts for?"

"Nobody knows for sure."

"But how do the Maidens continue if they take all the males?" asked Star.

"Some of the males are allowed to stay to keep the herd alive."

"But why don't they fight?"

"I think it is because it has always been that way," replied Nanuq.

"There is something else you need to know," said the bear gravely. "There are rumours of dark deeds surrounding these Guardians, though they are just the whispers across the wind."

"What whispers?" responded Star.

"Of sacrifice," said Nanuq.

"Sacrifice?" said Star.

"Yes, to the Gods. Some say this is why the young ones are never seen again."

Star looked out across the icy sea, and his heart suddenly felt very heavy. Somewhere inside himself, he had hoped perhaps that, here, away from the kind of evil that Shade was spreading, goodness would prevail. But now it seemed that he might encounter an even greater darkness.

"But how can that be? Then these Guardians are no better than Shade."

A chill went down the spine of the stallion. He considered this latest revelation. "But go I must, whatever there is to face, if it means I can rid the world of Shade and his ways."

Nanuq nodded as if he felt Star had made the right decision despite the added danger.

"One other thing young stallion. Those mountains are treacherous. Do not climb them at the time of the snows, it will likely kill you. If the storms come, you must go round. It is said that only Arion himself has ever climbed those peaks at this time."

The bear looked intently into the eyes of the horse. "Yes?"

Star nodded his agreement.

"Before I leave I must take some grass that grows in the sea. It's for a beaver I met. His mate is sick, and I promised I would bring some to him."

Star began collecting some seaweed.

"That stuff won't do you any good," said Nanuq, looking scornfully at the ground. "If she eats that it will only make her worse. You want the other kind," pointing his paw to the dry seaweed that Star had tasted before. "Over there."

"Thank you. Thank you very much," replied Star.

Nanuq gazed at the stallion. "Have you ever thought what the words of the Prophecy would mean if indeed you are the One?"

"Don't," cried the horse.

Star stared at the white bear, and once again he felt a fear well up inside, and Nanuq could see in the stallion's eyes that he had contemplated this thought, the magnitude of which was too much to comprehend. With this came anger, at everything that had happened to him. The anger made him feel stronger, and the bear could see a resolution begin to awaken in his mind.

"Nanuq. Thank you. It's time I left you. Kobet will be anxious."

A tinge of sadness played across the face of the wild bear, though he tried not to show it.

"Take care, Star. If you ever need me, send word via the birds, Migisi or whoever and I will come. One day I will be glad to hear how you fare and see if there's truth in this Prophecy."

Star picked up the seaweed in his mouth that had been collected earlier and walked from the beach.

The stallion headed back south as quickly as he could, laying down the seaweed only to graze and drink. When he reached Kobet's home on the river bank, the beaver was looking for him. The health of his mate had worsened. He took the seaweed, thanked Star and rushed to his lodge with the dangly stems.

Star spent the next few nights dozing by the river bank listening to the wind and the rushing water.

Though it reminded him a little, of the sea, he somehow knew that its nature was different.

The stallion woke one morning, and to his delight he found Kobet and his mate both sitting nearby, watching him. She seemed fully recovered.

"Thank you," she said shyly to the horse, "for helping us."

"Yes," said Kobet. "Now what can we do for you?"

Star smiled. "Nothing, I'm just pleased to have been able to help. But I should be on my way. I'm heading north-west beyond the big mountains. Which would be the best way?"

Kobet nodded. "Follow this river for two suns, then, take the left fork and follow that to the source. Eventually, you will see the mountains in the distance. Be careful my friend for the weather can be harsh there.

Star looked wistfully to the south where he thought his mother and friends now were, suffering who knew what fate, before turning north-west to continue his quest for truth.

"Star!" called Kobet. "We shall look out for you, all the beavers. We will not forget what you did. Always remember we are there for you. All animals will hear of your deeds. And Star, be careful we heard news along the river bank that some Zellats have even been spotted this far north. They are looking for something."

And with that Star disappeared into the distance.

Chapter 3

Star followed the river, and just as Kobet had said, he reached the fork on the dawn of the second sun.

As the stallion followed the river towards its source, he could see a range of mountains in the far distance and Star's mood swiftly sank. Loneliness crept in once more. He thought bitterly of his mother and friends and without knowing why, he began to feel the menace of Shade all around him and the threat of what lay ahead. What knowledge would he find there? Was the Prophecy real? More than that, what might he discover about himself? Would he be happy with the answers? These and other thoughts plagued his mind to the point where he began to talk to himself questioning and answering his queries all at once.

The land began to rise, and as he traversed the high slopes, he stopped and looked back and scented the breeze. But Star went on, rising higher and higher, instinctively avoiding the valley where occasional humans might be seen. However, of man or animal, for that matter, he saw little, for even if man did venture to this wilderness, there would be few places to find shelter.

Around him, the land became unfamiliar and foreboding. Huge forests rose up ahead of him, and cliff faces closed in. Waterfalls spewed out of the mist, and even the most isolated of places could not hide from the searching wind.

He was descending through a sparse wood to drink at a stream when he lifted his nose to the breeze. Horses! They were moving downwind and moving fast. Star's legs began to shake, and he felt a terrible apprehension in his stomach. He had not met another horse since he'd left the Chief's camp and while the stallion yearned for companionship, he also knew that the likelihood would be that they were with Shade.

Star bolted for the cover of the trees and waited. Six stallions came into view and halted some ten horse lengths away. Their coats were drenched in sweat and steam rose from their backs in the cold air.

"We're getting nowhere like this," said one of them wearily.

Star could hear them clearly in the stillness around. They hadn't seen him or sensed he was there.

"No, but we can't go back to Shade empty handed, can we?"

Star's senses were instantly on alert.

"It's your fault. We could have had them further back if you hadn't lost track of them…"

"Well, we can't stay out here. There's bound to be wolves around somewhere," interrupted a third. "Come on, we must keep looking!"

"Not sure what's worse, facing Shade with no prisoners or being torn limb from limb by a wolf," said another.

"Why does Shade want them so bad anyhow? They're quite young that lot."

"I think he wants the old one. You know the mother of that Prophecy thing everyone's on about. The one who died."

The horses moved away, leaving Star to ponder on his eavesdropping. His mind was a whirl with the revelation.

"My mother's alive, and it seems my friends too." His heart jolted. "Then they must be somewhere close."

The stallion felt hope swelling in his chest. Star stood for a moment waiting for the Zellats to move out of range, hardly able to contain himself.

"I must find them," said Star, turning up the hill, "and quickly."

By the next sun, Star had seen no signs at all of other horses. All day he had searched. The day stayed cold and damp. He was moving slowly along a ridge, checking for any clues when he felt his legs shaking. Then his whole body began to quiver. His nostrils filled with an overpowering scent that made him sick with fear.

Star twitched and peered around him. Then it came. An eerie chill ran through his body, a noise that took him back to that time before he met Migisi, the low, lonely howl of a wolf.

Then Star saw them standing sleek and strong, on a higher slope. Their silver fur bristled against the earth. They paced back and forth scenting the ground, then one of them lifted his head and spotted the stallion. The wolf howled, and the others raised their heads to his call. They too saw the horse, and their cries rose above the wind, their voices filled with hunger. Then without warning, they began to move, down the slope across a valley, towards the horse. Star turned and fled.

Though the wolves were far off and Star was fast, fear had him by the throat, and he ran blindly up the side of a hill. Panic took a hold. All he could think of was to escape. His senses were flooded with the stench of wolves, and terror had overcome him like a dark cloud. Instinct took over and no matter how hard he tried there was nothing he could do to suppress this fear. As he ran, he desperately fought to clear his mind, to plan a way out, but nothing came except his beating heart.

"Think!" he cried to himself, as the wolves called behind him, and he caught their scent again on the breeze, but poor Star could do nothing but flight.

At last, he began to tire and as he slowed he heard the rushing sound of water above, which distracted him and broke the spell. Star had climbed quite high and reached a waterfall that seemed to block his way. He stared at the cleft in the rock face, from which the white water raged out, the spray spattering on the sudden turn of the wind, lashing at him stinging his face and eyes.

To turn back now would be fatal. The pack closed in from all directions, scenting their quarry was trapped. Star's eyes darted about trying to find something. The slope above him became very steep and offered no way around the waterfall. His only route to possible safety was a narrow ledge, just wide enough to stand on, that ran behind the surging treacherous fall of white water, and he knew that if he slipped, if he faltered for a moment, he would be lost.

Star breasted the rush of icy water and its chill force almost took his legs away from him in the first moment. Then he gained some semblance of balance searching for secure footholds on the wet rocks. He slipped sideways, back towards the waterfall, scrambling desperately. Water and darkness engulfed him. Suddenly, he was through the torrent of water and still standing. The air was cold, and from the noise that thundered around him, he felt he was in the very centre of a raging storm.

There was no rest for Star, though, as two wolves had followed him behind the curtain of water, growling angrily. Gathering his thoughts, he quickly traversed along the ledge out to the other side.

To his horror, in front of him, poised, was a large male wolf. Star could see his menacing amber eyes, his snarling muzzle and sharp white teeth. His fur bristled along its throat.

"So, we meet again," snarled the wolf.

Star's eyes narrowed. "Goran?"

"Yes, my fine stallion. This time, you will not escape me."

Then a sharp crack sound pierced the still air. Goran was hurled sideways, yelping in pain, blood oozing from his rear leg.

The wolf pack scattered in panic, leaving their leader prostrate on the ground.

Star's instinct was to run also, but somehow he stayed. 'What happened?' he thought.

Goran lay helpless, his breathing rapid, his tongue hanging from the side of his mouth, whimpering in pain. Blood mingled and stained his fur, which pumped from the wound at each rasping gasp of breath.

Bemused, Star searched the horizon for a sign, but nothing immediate could be seen.

Then, from the cover of some nearby trees, emerged a strange creature covered in fur. It looked animal but walked on two feet and was carrying what appeared to be a long stick.

Instead of bolting to safety, however, which every sense in his body was urging Star to do, he felt strangely fearless. There was something familiar. It was human, white. He was clothed in fur and animal skins. The man's eyes fixed on Star as he moved closer and the horse saw compassion in his face, not the madness and hatred he had so far associated with these white people.

He was a trapper, a Frenchman, Pierre, who had lived in this area for many years. He had come to the wilderness to seek solitude. Star noticed his face was rugged and half covered by a thick black beard.

The stallion stayed and watched a few paces off as the man approached the wolf with caution. Goran snapped at the man but was unable to move without flinching in pain. Pierre removed a long sharp shiny object from a covering on his hip and Star was alerted to danger.

Instinctively, he moved forward to block the man's path to the wolf. The man stepped back a little, bemused at the apparent protective nature Star displayed towards the wolf. The hunter replaced his knife in his leather holster, nodding his agreement to stand down.

Pierre had spent many winters living a simple existence with nature and had come to view his kind through the eyes of the Native Indians, despising their greed and arrogance. So he had chosen this life of isolation from humankind, preferring the company of nature and the animals around.

The Frenchman approached Star cautiously. There was a profound peace about the man, and Star saw through his wild appearance. Pierre's eyes betrayed a caring soul, and the horse stood his ground, as the trapper's outstretched arm came closer. When his large rough hand stroked the stallion gently on his neck, Star felt a strange comfort that he had not experienced since the boy, and it warmed his heart.

"There, there," said Pierre as he caressed Star's neck. "You're a strange one, my beautiful stallion," he whispered, in a voice that felt as soft as the warmth of a summer sun.

He took out his blade again, and Star immediately reared in front of him his eyes flashing.

"Easy there. Easy…" urged Pierre.

"I'm not going to hurt anyone. But if it seems that you don't want me to kill this wolf, then I will need to take the bullet out and stop the bleeding."

Star calmed and stepped away.

Pierre collected wood and set about making a fire. The flame caught, and the trapper buried a second flat blade in the yellow inferno.

Goran felt threatened, baring his fangs, but too weak to defend himself.

"Goran," said Star. "This man is going to help you."

Goran hissed and growled. "He's human, he will kill me."

"If he were going to kill you he would have by now. You must trust me. Lie still."

Losing blood and unable to respond the wolf lay still while Pierre skillfully removed the bullet then taking the flat blade from the flames pressed it hard against the wound. Burning flesh and smoke billowed upwards, and Goran let out a roar that shook the mountains, before falling unconscious.

Star bolted to the safety of the trees and stayed there until darkness shrouded the valley.

Slowly, cautiously Star was drawn back to the crackling light of the campfire. Goran appeared to be still alive. Pierre watched over him tending to the wound and covering it with a poultice that smelt similar to the one Flying Hawk healed him with.

The Frenchman looked up at the horse who had strolled back to the campfire.

"This would be something to tell my children if I had any. A Mustang, a wolf and me around a campfire." He nodded and looked to the stars. "You're full of surprises. He's in your hands now." Pierre lay down by the fire musing at his situation.

Star also looked to the sky for answers, but the more he thought, the more confused he became. The stallion vowed to continue looking for his friends in the morning and reunite their small band again.

But morning came, and Pierre had vanished. The only evidence of his being there was the smouldering remains of the camp fire.

Though the smell of the wolf frightened Star, he stood there watching over the stricken creature. There were times during the day when Star tried to leave to look for his friends, but something kept calling him back.

Eventually, Goran opened his eyes. He whimpered sorrowfully and struggled to get up.

"Lie still," said Star.

Goran snarled at the horse, curling his upper lip so that the sharp canines stood out hard and white.

Star watched him warily, but even if Goran had been well enough to get up and spring at him, Star was far out of reach.

"Be still," called Star again.

"Come closer my fine stallion and I'll eat you," snapped Goran.

"That's no way to behave when I've just saved your life. That man would have killed you if I hadn't stopped him."

"This is no way for animals to behave," growled the wolf. "It's unnatural. It's against the law."

Star just watched.

"Why do you do this? Just leave me to die," muttered Goran angrily.

"What harm is there if one animal helps another?" said Star quietly.

"What harm? All the harm in the world, it's not right."

As night came again and a few stars peeped through the swirling clouds, the stallion came to see Goran again.

"How are you feeling?" he asked quietly.

The wolf licked the healing wound on his back leg and nodded.

"You saved my life," he said. "I'll be well soon."

"Then it's nearly time for me to leave," said Star.

"Yes, that is well," said Goran in a strange voice. "But tell me. I don't understand. Why you have done this?"

"Because you needed help," said Star quietly," and because I want to know."

"Want to know what?" said Goran.

"Many things. Who I am? Who you are? Why you hunt me?"

"Why I hunt you?" said the wolf licking his lips. "Because I want to run with the wind and have a full stomach. Because I want a mate with sleek, silver fur and I want my pack to howl their songs, and I also want to know…"

"Then tell me something about you," asked Star.

Goran looked oddly at the stallion, and then he nodded.

"Very well."

So Star settled and listened to the story the wolf had to tell. He heard of his leadership, his pack which ran free across the wilderness of America. He learned of the bitter winters. The times when they nearly starved when food was scarce.

Star listened intently and took in every detail of how wolves hunted and would fight over the spoils.

The stallion also heard of the She-wolf and the wolf's love of their young ones. He also heard of their loneliness, isolated from the world by the threat of man and his need to fight or die.

As he told Star, a deep stirring came to Goran. His fur bristled as he remembered his home, his family. He grew silent and sullen, and so the two animals were left listening to the rushing water and the whispering wind.

Then without warning the wolf rose to his feet and began to growl. His hair was standing up on the back of his neck, and suddenly he arched his spine and stared at the horse with malevolent menace.

Star back up a few steps. There was nowhere to run. "You're better then?" he said.

The wolf nodded and looked at Star slyly.

"I'm glad," said Star.

"Damn you!" howled Goran suddenly. "Why are you glad? Don't you know I could kill you here and now?"

"I'm glad all the same," said Star calmly. "I don't believe you will harm me, not today at least. The last time we met, even though you failed to catch me, you could have easily gone after my friends, but you kept your word. You have honour, my dear Goran."

The wolf let out a roar in frustration, for he knew the horse was right.

"No," he whispered bitterly. "I will not eat you."

"Then perhaps we have both learnt something these last few days. That even all men are not the same, that they are much like us in our world. As well as there is greed, there is compassion also."

"We have learnt nothing," snapped the wolf. "Except that the world is a stranger place than we thought. Now I suggest you leave this place before I change my mind."

Star nodded. "Very well, but I will not forget this time we spent together Goran. Goodbye…"

Star turned and galloped up the slope, and when he looked back from a ledge above, there was a moment's respect from each of them. The stallion swung round to leave, and the wolf called to him.

"Listen to me," he howled. "You saved my life, and for that I thank you. So go, run free like the Mustang you are. I will not forget you either but do not fool yourself, for we are enemies, you and I. That is how it is and will always be. Nothing may change that, for that is the law. So when I am with my family again, and our stomachs are empty, and my cubs grow hungry, I will hunt you. Then I will forget this strange meeting. Yes, and glad to forget it too."

Goran was snarling now as he tried to master his instinct to kill. Without another word, Star disappeared from the ledge and set off in his pursuit of his friends and mother.

Only when Star had a clear distance between himself and the wolf did he look back and ponder what had happened and the strange bond he appeared to have formed with his arch enemy. Then, on the drifting breeze, Star heard his cry, haunting and beautiful. Instead of fear, the stallion felt a strange warmth come to him. Star looked out over the barren wilderness. The clouds and mist hung low over the day, and their dark edges were thick with rain. On he went. But as he went something else came with the biting loneliness that descended to greet him, a terrible sadness.

Chapter 4

The weather was changing rapidly now as Star travelled further north-west, towards the mountain range. The stallion kept a keen eye out for any signs of his mother and the others.

His journey was slow. This land was more water than earth. Water lay everywhere, in shallow oblong lakes with rivers and streams that meandered endlessly to nowhere. Walking was torture, and the rain seemed never to stop so that when the skies did clear for a while, grumbling with thunder, Star felt as though he had been swimming against a strong river current that had soaked through to his bones.

With the time of the red moon approaching, clouds of biting and sucking insects plagued the stallion. He hated this place and longed to reach higher ground.

Star finally swung west, following the contours of the hills. Great splinters of rock rose around him now. Stone screes scarred the land, and the mountain range loomed ever higher through the hanging mist.

It was morning, and Star was following the shoreline of another lake. The hillside soared steep and plunged sheer to the water, and all around they rose up again in walls of stone. The weather turned cold, lashing the surface of the lake. Little was the stallion to know that this was just a taste of the bitter winter that was coming.

Along the way, Star found some fresh hoof marks on the muddy ground. Taking a closer look, he realised that they weren't just mares but stallions as well. He raised his head to the air trying to scent for a clue, but nothing came on the wind to help direct him. Knowing they could not be too far ahead, he decided to pick up his pace, and it wasn't long before he spotted them in the distance, through the mist. There were six of them, grazing together. Star's heart began to race.

*****

"I'm s-s-soaked through," said Chub miserably, as he stood there in the rain. The mist swirled around the little group of horses. The fat little skewbald had grown into a fine stallion.

"I know, Chub, it's horrid," said a mare next to him. Ella had blossomed, into a beautiful palomino mare. Her smooth coat was the colour of toffee gold, and her ivory white mane glinted even in this dull light.

"T-T-Tarn never stops grumbling," said Chub, looking towards the young stallion who was talking to Armand and Misty. They had changed since their escape from Shade over a year before. Misty looked the spitting image of her sister, and both Tarn and Armand had matured into formidable horses.

"Yes," agreed Ella. "I'm worried about him. He hates the Zellats, but I think he hates running from them even more."

"Yes," neighed Chub, but then he added, "but when Tarn decided to escape with us he did throw his whole heart into it. I doubt we would have made it this f-f-far without him."

"He is developing into a natural leader, I know, but sometimes I feel he's too aggressive," pondered Ella.

"I-I-I'm concerned about Bruma. Her leg's worsening. It's slowing us up terribly."

They both looked across to where Bruma was standing, grazing half-heartedly across the soggy ground. Her leg had been wounded just over two moons before, and it still wasn't healing.

"I-I-I still think she suffers over Star," said Chub.

Both of them hated to think of that horrible day when the buffalo came.

Ella gazed into the mist.

"I miss him terribly," she muttered quietly.

"M-M-Me too," nodded Chub.

Ella affected a cheerful smile. "We should keep going."

Chub began to move towards the others but then suddenly stopped dead. The stallion lifted his head to the horizon, his eyes searching for something.

Ella noticed his concern. "What is it Chub?"

"I-I-I don't know." I th-th-think it's another horse."

"Zellats?" whispered Ella, staring fixedly through the gloom.

Suddenly, a gust of wind cleared the mist away, and the two of them saw a stallion running towards them. But Ella, whose eyes were sharper, was shaking and shaking uncontrollably.

"E-E-Ella," whispered Chub, "what's the matter."

"It can't be."

"W-w-what?"

Both horses focused on the on-coming stallion, a growing realisation building in them of the impossible recognition of who it seemed to be.

"It can't be…" said Ella hardly daring to breathe.

Chub now was trembling. "I-i-impossible."

But as the stallion drew closer Ella could see for sure. Then Ella broke into a canter and sped towards him, as fast as she could.

"Star!" she neighed, "Star, you're alive!"

The emotion was electric. Star returned from the dead, surrounded by this small party of horses, themselves at their nerves' end from their escape. Star's own unbounded joy, all blended to produce an overwhelming mixture of exhilaration and wonder.

They could hardly stop talking, the friends quizzing Star about everything that had happened to him and marvelling at his account of his time at the Camp, his meeting again with Goran and Nanuq.

Star asked them about Leonardo, Morro and their capture and escape, which confirmed Nanuq's version of events. The group had so many questions to ask they hardly had time to discuss where exactly they were going. Star brought a sober reality back to the situation by informing them that Zellats were close, and it would be better if they continued talking as they travelled.

So the friends set off once more, and Chub explained proudly how they had escaped from Shade and his Zellats and how they had wandered in different directions to avoid the Zellats before finally being able to turn north. The going had been desperately slow, with the countryside being full of the enemy and trying to encourage Bruma to keep up. So they spent much of this time hiding during the day, trying to travel more through the night to avoid detection.

Star's reunion with his mother was very moving. When the stallion first approached Bruma, she looked quizzically into his face, and as she stared into his deep eyes, only the faintest flicker of recognition came into her sad eyes, mingled with a note of fear.

"Mother, it's me," Star whispered gently. The stallion licked and nuzzled her and tried to tease her from her stupor.

Bruma said nothing as she listened and Star knew that she barely understood him. Her wounded leg caused concern, and he set about looking for some herbal leaves he had seen used with Goran and very gently, began rubbing some of it into the cut.

Armand, Chub, Ella and Misty could hardly contain their joy at Star's reappearance, all except Tarn that is. He was a little colder than the rest, though he tried to hide it. He listened to Star's story carefully, but after they had travelled a couple of suns, it was almost like old times, as though they had never parted. Bruma stayed very close to Star but still spoke little.

It was then that each one shared their plans, and Star told the group of the mysterious Guardians of

Arion that lived beyond the western mountains. "Nanuq said that they might have answers for me."

"About the Prophecy?" said Ella quietly.

There was a silent pause. Each one looked around nervously. No one had expected Ella to have mentioned it so openly, but each of them had secretly wanted to ask Star. They had been waiting for a chance to get him alone. But Ella, knowing more of Star's heart than the others, wanted to bring it out into the open as quickly as possible. Star knew what they were all thinking.

"I'm not sure the Prophecy is true? Can it be true, Mother?" he murmured, looking to Bruma.

She looked back suddenly, with a fearful glance, but said nothing and Star went on. "But maybe parts of it are, and there are some who believe this as fact. These Guardians that Nanuq spoke of should know something."

"Th-Th-Then you'll need some good companions to keep you company on the journey then," stuttered Chub.

"I can't expect you to come where I'm going. It's likely to be dangerous," replied Star.

"Well that's just great, Star," came Ella's terse response. She paced about irritated. "If you think you can get rid of us that easily then you're mistaken. Besides, you're not the only one who can look after themselves you know," she snorted.

"We'd be stronger together," added Armand.

Star nodded. "Then we should get some rest, for whatever we will find there, we daren't stay here much longer. It's not safe."

Star felt a moment of pride and happiness. His friends were here, and their companionship gave him a sense of safety that he had not had in a long while.

Chapter 5

It was mid-morning when the horses got on their way. The weather was colder than it had been. A hard frost made the grass spark and glitter. After a time, on their journey north-west, they ventured into a large valley. Steepling cliffs and jagged rock peaks reached skywards about them. They headed on towards the edge of a lake that they could now see ahead of them in the distance, finally reaching it after a sun's trek.

Star pulled them up as they came close to the end of the lake. In the distance, spreading out from the edge of the water, they saw three wooden dwellings. Wisps of smoke curled gently into the sky.

"This is white man's place," muttered Star to himself but rather than feel agitated the scene curiously calmed him.

The others though stirred as the scent of humans came to them across the wind, but Star told them not to worry, for they were still far away. Star could see, though, that to travel ahead would bring them too close, and although part of him thought that these humans posed no danger, his natural instinct still alerted him towards flight. Caution did get the better of him, so he decided to turn back and strike a new route through the valley and soon the horses were entering the valley's broad flanks.

A strange hush fell over the group as they walked. The terrain around them was so different from the Prairies of their home. They felt they were entering a world of dreams as the vast walls of the valley stood like sleeping giants. The track they were taking twisted left and right through the hills, following a river gurgling through its centre.

Ahead loomed three great spurs of rock and the rich, dark green of the valley and the slate black of the hillsides seemed to swallow them up. Soon they felt like tiny moving specks lost in an immensity of stone. High above them, the cry of birds echoed against the dizzy crags, and the mist swayed and broke across the trees.

In the late afternoon, they crossed the river, and the sun managed to break through the clouds. Their spirits rose for the valley had grown eerily beautiful under its gentle light. They came to a smaller lake but didn't pause to drink as they felt an urgency to press on, as though something was chasing them. The sombre mystery that hung about the place made the horses tremble and start at the slightest sound so that by the time night came down they were at their nerve's end.

"Do you feel it?" whispered Ella, to Star, breathlessly, as they stopped in the twilight.

"Yes," said Star, there's something strange about the place, a familiar feeling. I don't know what it is yet."

"C-c-could it be these Guardians you spoke of?" queried Chub.

"No, I don't think so, and I don't sense anything like that," answered Star. "But it's very odd. Like some feeling far away, that I've had before."

Chub looked nervously at his friend.

The group went on as silently as before. The darkness turned the crags and the stones into fearful shapes, and the air seemed to hold an impossible stillness. With the night, it began to rain again and soon the horses were miserable. They stopped to graze a little and then huddled together in the shadow of the hills. At last, Star suggested that they move on, so the horses crept ahead through the darkness as the wind wailed through the valley. They began to imagine that they were part of the old tales that Halden the storyteller would speak to them of, of Gods and legends that ran with the stars and even Arion himself.

After a while, however, Star started to grow restive again and kept stopping to scent the air or listen to the wind. But it was a good while before they heard a sound that made them all stop in their tracks. It rose strange and mournful, around the rocks. The horses crowded together and listened, and when it stopped, finally and suddenly, Star nodded.

"I thought so," he whispered. "There are more humans ahead. But they are not the white faced ones."

"What shall we do?" asked Armand. "Go back?"

Star looked quizzically towards the camp. "I think we should go on. If we stay here or go back, we could easily run into Zellats."

"But they're humans," said Tarn.

There was something inside Star telling him it was safe. He turned to the others. "What do you all think?"

"We will follow you Star," said Ella confidently, despite their fear of humans.

Tarn's expression showed concern but acceptance for the decision.

They were preparing to set off when Bruma suddenly spoke. It was the first thing she had said since the reunion.

"I don't think I can," she said hoarsely. "I think I'll stay here."

"But you can't, Mother," said Star.

"Just leave me, I'll be right. I'll come in the sunlight. You wait ahead for me up there."

"No, Mother," said Star firmly. He could see she was shaking badly. "It will be fine, I know it will."

But Bruma just shook her head and said desperately, "Just leave me. Can't you see I don't want to come yet?"

Star looked Bruma tenderly in the eyes and began to speak quietly.

"We're all afraid, Mother. But it will be far more dangerous to stay here on your own. Everything will be fine. The humans will be asleep, and they will not harm us. You have to trust me."

Bruma shook her head.

"I can't. It's as though everything around me is black."

"I know. It's as though you are trapped, but you can control it. Fight the blackness until you can think again. That's the secret, Mother. Follow closely in my tracks, and I will lead you through. Think of something special, anything. As long as you can think, it will be all right."

Bruma looked at Star pleadingly, but at last, she nodded.

"Right, listen to me, all of you. I know something of these people, so I will lead. Stay close and do what I do. Walk slowly if I do, run if I run. I will take us around them if I can, and tomorrow we'll be away from here."

The young stallion nodded resolutely, turned and led them on.

Above them, the sky began to rumble, and it started to rain. The water came down in torrents, great pebbles of wet so that the horses were soon soaked and the ground began to turn to mush as the water splashed and slurried down the sides of the valley. After a while, they dimly made out the source of their fear.

The tepees, only ten or so, were grouped together in a narrowing part where the surrounding hills closed in to form a barrier, which made it impossible for the horses to skirt around them on this side. Ella and the others fully expected Star to stop and lead them across the river and across to the opposite side of the valley. But the stallion did nothing of the kind, hardly slowing once or turning round to reassure the others. Star led them off the slopes and straight towards the encampment.

As the strange smells hit their nostrils, there was not one of the other horses who did not want to turn and run. Each of them felt it. Fear came over them like a fog, but they remembered what Star had said and struggled to keep the feeling at bay. Star's strange calmness as he walked ahead gave each of them confidence.

The tepee encampment was still. The dying embers of a large open fire spat and fizzled their last, as the drumming cacophony of rain drowned out everything. Star began to lead his group along a natural pathway through the middle of the dwellings, their heads hung low as they squelched through the mud, hardly daring to breathe.

Bruma, who was in the midst of the group, kept looking back nervously at Ella behind her. Although the mare was herself petrified, she nodded to Bruma calmly and kept going without a sound. A horse whinnied mournfully from somewhere, and a dog began to bark, but Star neither ran nor quickened his pace. At last the tepees began to disappear behind them as the party moved on.

Only then did Star suddenly thrown back his head and gallop up the slope of the valley. The others followed him instantly, and soon they were all racing away as fast as their legs could carry them.

"Star, you got us through," whinnied Ella delightedly.

To her surprise, Star didn't answer her. He just kept on going, straight ahead through the soaking grass. He didn't stop for ages, and when he did so, he still said nothing, but looked about him desperately.

The friends began to talk amongst each other, adrenaline and a sense of relief overpowering their skittish behaviour. Only Star stayed apart, at the crest of a hill, looking back across the valley to the camp. Ella ambled up to him slowly.

"Star," she murmured, "Star, what is it? What's wrong?"

Still, he said nothing.

"Star, please tell me, you're frightening me."

Star flinched and seemed to come out of a reverie.

"Ella," he said, his eyes clearing, "is it you?"

"Yes. What is it, Star? Can I help you?"

"No, I don't think so," said Star bitterly, "It's something to do with that camp, maybe it's this place, I don't know. A feeling I can't get rid of. Ella, I'm afraid."

"We are all afraid, Star, but it's gone now. You led us through. You know Star, it's right what you said about fighting the feeling and thinking at all costs. There was a point out there when…"

"No Ella, I'm still afraid and confused. The feeling's still in me. It's got something to do with that place down there." The stallion's head gestured to the far off camp.

"When we came to the humans, I thought at first that we should cross the valley to the other side and try to avoid them, but something took hold of me. I don't know what it was. Something was drawing me closer to them again. I think to learn more about them, I don't know, curiosity. I was right at first, walking through their camp, but as we went something else happened. Something new came over me."

"What, Star?"

"I was listening very intently for any noise that meant we should run. Then, I suddenly thought I could hear the humans, breathing all around me. Then I knew they were asleep in their shelters. But there was something familiar there also. As I concentrated, everything around me suddenly began to grow light, and it wasn't raining anymore. The path we were on was dry and as I looked up a mist was rolling towards me across the valley. But, Ella," said Star trembling violently now, his voice strangled with pain, "the mist was made of blood. The whole camp was red, and as it came down, I suddenly felt a terrible pain. It was linked to those sleeping bodies around us. But there was something else. Some feeling that I couldn't touch, like anger. Then suddenly my ears were filled with screams and the air was thick with the smell of death. I looked up and realised that we had come to the edge of the camp, and I began to run."

"Star," whispered Ella, "how horrible. Maybe something happened here."

Star thought for a while. "I don't know. I can see more clearly now, but I need to think for a while. Alone, if that's all right."

Ella nodded and left Star to himself. She went back to the group who were grazing quietly. Armand and Chub enquired about their friend. Ella just shook her head and told them not to worry. After a while, the mare closed her eyes and began to doze. When she woke, Star was still standing at the same spot.

She allowed Star some time alone before returning to his side, sensing his need for companionship. She said nothing at first but just gazed out over the land into the approaching morning. The soaring valley became shrouded in a thick mist that hung heavily in its bottom and made it look strange and peaceful.

"I'm all right," muttered Star quietly.

"I think we should be on our way," said Ella kindly.

Star nodded, but Ella could see that he was in no state to lead them. So she went up to Chub and whispered something in his ear. He understood immediately.

"C-c-come on, everyone," Chub cried cheerfully, "It's t-t-time to go and if you don't mind I w-w-want to lead."

"You lead?" snorted Tarn. He would have argued had Ella not silenced him with her eyes and nodded to where Star was standing.

So Chub led the horses away in the misty dawn as the light swelled the valley. Chub, Armand, Tarn and Misty were trotting on ahead while Star and Ella hung behind with Bruma, trailing them. As they went, Star kept stopping and looking back through the mist.

"Ella," he murmured, "I think I understand now. I know why I wasn't sure about the danger. It's because it has nothing to do with us. It was about them. Humans, I mean."

"What did you see?" asked Ella.

"Death," said Star quietly. "I saw death and pain, betrayal and suffering."

Star looked intently at the mare.

"But it's all right. It is not our fear."

"And the red mist and the vision?" whispered Ella. "Something happened to them?"

Star was silent at first, and when he spoke, he was looking back at the encampment.

"Yes, Ella and somehow I felt connected to it," he answered softly. Star was staring hard now, and his eyes were glassy. "And there will be more pain to come."

With that, Star shook his mane and turned. He led Ella and Bruma away from that place.

*****

The camp stirred after a fitful night's sleep. A few squaws went about their business, gathering firewood and water. A young brave emerged from his tepee, wrapped tightly in animal furs to protect him from the bitter morning chill.

His face was lined beyond his age, and his eyes betrayed a sense of sadness that sat deep in his heart. His father, the Chief, had made the decision years ago to accept the white man's treaty and took his people to the Trading Post reservation.

Disease and hunger had taken its toll. Chief Brown Elk died of a broken heart, and his son Flying Hawk was determined that his people would not suffer the same fate.

The brave had remembered his act of kindness to a friend of his, a horse he let go, all those years ago and he thought also, it would be better to live free than to die in that place of sorrow.

One night, he led what remained of his Lakota tribe away, on a long journey north, out of his native lands, which eventually brought him here, to the Land of the Great Mother and the redcoat soldiers, modern day Canada.

Chased by bounty hunters and bluecoats, few survived the arduous trip. Many of the old and sick either perished in the harsh winter or died at the hands of their bloodthirsty trackers.

But make it they did, across the border, but the price of their freedom was high. At least here, in this new place, they were not hunted like animals. Here at least they had a chance once more. Life's challenges would be hard, but it would be on their terms.

Flying Hawk, had not slept well that night, but it was not the raging storm that had kept him awake, something else occupied his thoughts. Something he had not felt for a while, a longing he had tried to forget, a stallion that had once touched his heart.

He felt a strange closeness once more. His thoughts took his gaze to the far off horizon as if searching for something, a presence. The glow of the rising sun cut through the clinging mist, and once more he felt a connection. He looked to the sky.

"Oh, great Wakan Tanka, watch over us, and I pray someday my friend, and I will meet once more."

Chapter 6

The group maintained a north-westerly direction as the weather became noticeably colder with the progression of the season. The days grew shorter and birds prepared for their migration south. Fear gripped the horses as they knew they were rising to meet it, for every sun grew a little colder.

It was about seven suns since their encounter with the human camp, and they woke one early morning to find their coats dusted with a powdery sprinkling of snow.

They had reached a high span of hills, part of the mountain range that they were heading for and began to climb. Soon they were above the tree line and here shelter was hard to find from the winds that had started to batter the other sides of the mountain. At this moment they were still below the snowline for recently, the tops of the mountain had been draped with a thick cloak of white.

Star and his companions struggled, unbeknown to them, towards what was destined to be one of the hardest seasons ever seen in this region. The wind changed suddenly, turning its breath on the eastward side of the mountain and they felt the cold grip of air with a new threat that made the horses shiver even under their thickening coats. The skies above grew heavy, so heavy that it felt as if it would press the mountain flat with the weight of the ice congealing in the heavens.

They could feel nature's danger settling all around them. When the clouds finally opened, instead of the interminable, drenching rains that turned the land into a soggy mush, the crisp air was suddenly sharp with huge snowflakes that piled quickly and thick on the earth, and the horses were soon turned into moving smudges on a sheet of white.

On they went until the snow stopped and the morning brought them off the slopes down into another valley, its patterns and forms lost under the sweeping white. It stretched ahead, flat as a sigh, before rising again into the arms of a mountain that seemed to climb higher than anything about it. On its tops and flanks, the snows were heavy, and high above, the wind lashed across the white.

As Star looked up, he shivered.

"The Great Mountain," he whispered to himself.

They deliberated for most of the day what to do next, scraping at the hard ground to get to the sparse nourishment beneath. There wasn't one of them that didn't feel a strange sense of awe and foreboding as they hovered in the shadows of the mountain, for they were in the land of their stories, of myths and legends.

Star had drifted away from the group and was trying to feed on a clump of vegetation when he suddenly heard a noise. As he looked up through the bushes he spied a face, watching him intently; a pair of large eyes in a smudge of brown. The face suddenly vanished.

"Who's there?" called Star.

The bushes rustled, and a young bay horse stepped nervously out in front of Star. The young horse began to shake.

Star sensed the fear. "Don't be frightened. I won't harm you."

The young horse looked terrified and said nothing.

"Come, it's all right. What's your name?"

"Erith," said the horse at last in a tiny high pitched voice.

"Well Erith," said Star, "pleased to meet you."

Erith remained cautious, head lowered.

"Look, Erith, you don't need to be afraid." Star's kind eyes fixed on the youngster.

"Are you with Him?" replied the horse nervously.

"Him? What do you mean?"

"Shade."

Star recoiled from the name. "Shade is here?"

"Well, his Zellats are everywhere. I thought you might be one of them."

"Then why are you out here on your own?"

"I'm not on my own. Our Band or should I say many Bands are sheltering in a valley to the south of here. I'm a look out," said Erith proudly.

"You're a little small to be a Band scout, aren't you?" probed Star, searching for the real truth.

Erith sighed, "I'm not a scout, I'm just exploring. I shouldn't be here really. If my mother found out, she'd…" Erith looked at Star with pleading eyes.

A warm compassion came over the stallion, remembering his rebellious youth back on his home Prairie.

"Don't worry, it will be our secret, I won't tell anyone."

The young horse exhaled a relieved gasp.

"You said that there are many of you here, young Erith? How many?"

"There are maybe up to a hundred. We have all come north to escape. We are too many for the Zellats at the moment, so we are safe. We had planned to cross the mountains, but with the snow coming, the herd decided to stay in the valley until the great thaw."

Star pondered this opportunity, glancing up at the menacing mountain range. He shivered and felt a strange stirring in his guts, like a kind of longing.

"Will you not join us?" said Erith, his intonation pressing for a name.

"Thank you, but I will push on I think, across the mountains. There are answers I seek that cannot wait."

"But to cross at this time, is so dangerous," said Erith.

"I have no time to wait. I go to find the Guardians." Star nodded his thanks.

"Guardians?"

"Yes. They are supposedly the protectors of the Prophecy, young Erith."

"But the Prophecy can't be real, he's dead." Erith lowered his head.

"Perhaps you should go back to your mother before you end up running into those Zellats. My name is Star, by the way."

The young horse pondered the name approvingly, then, as it sank into his mind his eyes sprang open. "Star! The Star? You… It's you, the one everyone speaks of, the Prophecy?" Erith staggered back as if he had seen a ghost. "It can't be." The young horse was unable to contain his excitement.

"Whether I am of the Prophecy I do not know."

"But Shade told everyone you were dead, that buffalos killed you."

"It is true I nearly died that day, but I was saved, by a young human." Star's mind drifted to the fond memories of his time with Flying Hawk.

"Human! I can't wait to tell the herd everything. It will give us hope again. I will take my leave now, Star, and thank you. May Arion be with you." Erith turned excitedly and galloped away, throwing his head back in happy recognition of his meeting.

Star stood there momentarily as he watched the young horse disappear, before looking to the lonely summit of the mountain.

"Am I the One? Will I finally find out my purpose?" he whispered, before he too turned and ran back to his friends.

When he reached them, they were gathered together, discussing the journey and the best route to follow.

"We'll have to skirt its flanks," Tarn was saying. "It would be far too dangerous with the snows coming, to try and climb it. Best to find a way round."

"Star," said Ella as he came up, "Tarn thinks we should try to skirt the mountain and find a way round, keep to the foothills to avoid the cold."

"Yes, that would be a good route for you. Or you could wait until the geese come back. There is a herd to the south of here. I've just met one of them. Perhaps you should all stay with them. You will at least be safe there."

"What do you mean by you?" said Ella.

"I'm going to climb it," said Star quietly, looking up.

"B-b-but you can't," cried Chub.

"I'm going to try."

"But why?" pressed Ella.

"Because it will be quicker. If I'm ever going to discover the truth, I need to know now. I can't wait another season. There is not time and too much suffering. If I can indeed make a difference, then I must take that chance. With every moon that passes, Shade gains more control."

The others were aghast. What Star was contemplating was terribly dangerous.

Star continued. "You will be safe from the Zellats, with the herd to the south of here and we can meet up when the warm season comes…"

"Well," interrupted Chub. "If that's what you've decided. I'm c-c-coming with you."

"And me," added Armand enthusiastically. "What a story that would make for my little ones."

"No!" snorted Star. "I've got to do this alone. Besides, I've put you in enough danger already."

"I'm coming as well," said Ella.

"No, Ella."

Ella faced Star defiantly. "If you think I'm going to leave now I've only just found you again, you're wrong."

"Can I come as well?" said Misty, looking fondly at Chub. The stallion almost blushed.

Star's gaze fell on each of them, and he realised how deeply fond he was of them all.

"We'll all go," said Ella, "if that's what you want to do. Besides, if we try to go round, who knows where the Zellats will be waiting for us. One thing's for sure, they won't be up there."

But Star held his ground.

"Tarn, tell them they're being foolish," he said, looking suddenly towards his mother. "There's much less chance of us all crossing and mother will never make it."

Tarn nodded.

"If you don't want to stay with the other herd then Tarn can lead you around somehow," said Star.

"No," said Armand, "Tarn can take your Bruma round if he wants, but I'm determined."

The others agreed. Star tried to argue, but they kept insisting and after a while his resistance began to break down. But then something happened that decided it for all of them.

"Look," Armand suddenly shouted to the others.

"There!" cried, Misty.

In the distance, from two sides, a dozen or so Zellats were coming straight towards them.

"Zellats!" snorted Star bitterly. "Quickly!"

There was only one choice for them to escape now and that meant straight up.

Chapter 7

The clouds were thick with snow as they fled up the sides of the mountain. A wind came up too, which blew hard into their faces and the thought of what dangers lay ahead, and the Zellats close on their hooves soon subdued their spirits. Great dense snowflakes began to fall and very quickly the small group could hardly see the next horse ahead of them, as they sank deeper and deeper into the cold white. The wind grew fierce as they bunched together instinctively for protection. Within just a little while, the blizzard had become so intense that they could hardly make any headway at all. The storm, though, had at least masked them from the pursuing Zellats.

They came to a great spur of rock with scraggy trees above them, and they were forced to swing in a different direction. In the blizzard, they didn't know that they were now travelling along a narrow ridge that dropped dangerously away to their right. The ground was quite steep, and the horses slipped and stumbled, their forelegs sinking into the snow so that they were forced to kick and jump to make any progress at all. The falling snow swirled in blinding flurries, and the bitingly cold wind tore at the horses as they inched painfully up the slopes. Several times they came close to the edge of the spur, and it was only by luck that stopped one of the horses slipping and crashing down onto the rocks below.

Eventually, the mountain flattened out a little. It was here that Star found a place that offered some temporary shelter. Hardly a cave, but a rock overhang where the wind had scooped out the newly fallen snow, creating a kind of snow pit below the stone lip. There was plenty of room for them all, and they grouped together for warmth for a while, shivering in the hollow, their thickening coats flecked with white, the frost rising around their nervous breath.

It suddenly stopped snowing as quickly as it had started, revealing the dangerous path they had just taken. To their horror, they saw that at one point, they had crossed an outcrop of frozen snow which seemed to have nothing supporting it at all.

As the horses pressed on they found themselves on the edge of a pass with a clear stretch of firm, open snow banking not too steeply above them, which was crisp and hard under foot. They began to climb, and after a while, a thin sun even managed to pierce the clouds and offered brittle warmth to them all.

The sun didn't last, and as they reached the top of the defile where the slope above them opened further, it started to snow again. With the snow came a wind whose breath had been hardened on the mountain top. Worse than this, though, the horses had now reached the ice line where the fallen powder had compacted and turned hard and glassy. Their feet began to skitter and slip across the solid ground. Lower down the mountain the going had been so hard because of the depth of snow, and Star and his companions sunk into it nearly up to their haunches, but now they found they could hardly get a purchase on the ground at all. Several times they slipped and at one point Misty, who had climbed higher than the others, lost her footing and might have been injured if her slide back down the slope had not been blocked by a painful collision with Armand.

It was Ella who had the idea of threading across the ice face then turning back a little higher up so that they ended up zigzagging back and forth. In this way, the horses managed to climb. But a new danger confronted them, for traversing the steep slope like this brought them to the edge of small ravines and sudden drops with no precise definition in the snow. The horses could not see them until they were right on top of them. Several times, Star nearly came to grief, only to see the danger just in time.

The higher they got, the colder it became and as the day wore on the wind grew more and more fierce. When they were trying to move into its path, as it blew from one direction across the slope, they felt like twigs that could be snapped in two at any moment. But when they traversed back again, they found they were forced forward too quickly to keep a firm foothold on the ice. Worst of all, night was now coming in. The darkness came suddenly, and with the moaning wind swirling through their heads, there wasn't one of them who didn't tremble. Except for the weak Bruma whose leg had got worse and who was so exhausted that she could hardly think at all.

Misty, who was travelling with her, suddenly called out to her.

"Bruma, Bruma, you're wandering off."

The mare had just started to drift down the slope.

"What?" she muttered, in a dreamy voice. "I'm sorry, I'm so sleepy I can hardly keep awake."

"You must, Bruma," cried Misty.

"I know. But it's so hard. I keep thinking I'm there on the Prairie with the sun on my back."

Misty shivered as a blast of snowy wind whistled round her head.

Just as Bruma had spoken, they were interrupted by the terrifying squeal of a stallion ahead. It was Star. By the time they got to him, he was pounding the ice with his hooves.

"What is it?" cried Misty.

Chub shook his head at his friend.

"Armand, what's happened?" shouted Misty, but now she could see at least part of the cause of Star's distress, for he had come to the edge of a cliff.

"Ella," gasped Star.

Misty looked around, and to her horror, she realised that her sister had vanished. Just in front of them, where the ground suddenly dropped away into the void, the snow was marked and scuffed where Ella, blind and cold, had slipped and fallen over the edge.

"No!" squealed Misty bitterly.

The friends inched forward and stared out stupidly over the drop. They saw little, as the snowflakes swirled and scurried thick before their eyes.

"Ella," sobbed Star, "Ella, what have I done?"

Misty and the others began to call, but they heard and saw nothing from below. They fell silent, numbed by cold and loss. The wind moaned as though the spirits of a thousand horses were feeling the pain and rage that rose in their hearts. Ella was gone. But still, they stayed where they were until Bruma's eyes began to mist over with pain. It was Armand who came to his senses first and none too soon.

"Star!" cried Armand, "we must keep moving. If we stay here, we're sure to die. Look at your mother, she can hardly stand up."

Star said nothing. He was still staring out hopelessly over the drop.

"Star, this is no time to give up. What would Ella have said?"

Star lifted his head and looked longingly at his friend. Then he nodded gravely.

"Yes," he whispered, "yes Armand, you're right. We must get moving. Listen to me, all of you. We've got to keep going. There'll be time to mourn Ella later."

Tarn was the first to move, but as Star started to follow the others, Armand stopped him.

"Bruma," he whispered.

Bruma was still standing there, looking out over the drop. Her whole body was shaking.

"Mother!" cried Star over the wind, "you've got to come."

Bruma made no answer.

"Mother, please. There's nothing we can do."

"What's wrong?" shouted Armand.

"She won't move," said Star desperately.

"Bruma. Can you hear me?" said Armand. It's me, Armand."

Star dropped his muzzle and began to nudge her in the side. It swung his mother slightly to the right, but the mare seemed to hear and see nothing. Star's nudges got stronger, but they still had no effect in rousing her.

"Mother," pleaded Star, almost at his wits' end. "Can you hear me? If you…"

But with that Bruma turned her head slightly.

"Quiet," she said suddenly, "listen."

The two stallions pricked up their ears scanning for something, but all they heard was the howling fury of the night. Star shook his head sadly.

"Nothing."

"Just the wind," agreed Armand.

"No, wait," said Star suddenly. "What's that?"

The wind had died a little again, and as Armand strained to listen, he too thought that he heard a faint voice. Their senses were on full alert now, and Misty had joined them. For a while, their hopes fought the wind and faded as the sound they thought they had heard, was lost again below the mountain's angry cry. Then suddenly the wind dropped almost entirely, and the horses were sure. Below them, they could hear something calling. It was a mare calling Star's name.

"Ella," cried Star.

"Star. Star, is that you?" came the voice.

"Ella. Where are you? I can't see you."

"I'm below you, I think. But I can't see you either."

"Are you hurt?" shouted Star.

"No, Star just a little bruised. The snow broke my fall. I think I was very lucky, though. There are rocks everywhere. But Star, I've found a cave. We could shelter. It's dry."

"Cave," whispered Armand. "Thank Arion."

"But Ella, how do we reach you?" cried Star.

"I don't know," said Ella. "I've tried moving along the slope to find a way back up, but it's too dark, and the snow is very deep."

In fact, the snow was getting deeper, and the storm was intensifying. The group's relief of Ella's safety was soon lessened by the realisation that their situation was, if anything, worse than before. For now, they were separated from Ella by a good drop and no matter how hard they tried, they could not find a way down. Star sent Armand and Tarn to scout ahead and behind them, but they soon returned to report that the weather was now so bad that to search along the edge of the ridge would be fatal.

Star tried desperately to think of a way out, but nothing came to him. The night wore on, and the air began to freeze. High above them the wind, caught in rock fissures and caves, howled mournfully like the ghosts of horses past were coming to claim them.

Ella began to grow more and more worried for her friends, for at least below them she was protected from the full brunt of the storm. She tried to persuade Star and the others to move on without her, but they refused and soon they were so cold and wet that they couldn't have made it very far anyway. The others grouped together and very quickly became white, as heaped snow settled on them, their forms taking on the resemblance of ethereal statues.

Only Star stood alone, talking less and less frequently to Ella, hoping in vain that some idea would come to him to save them from the mountain.

He lifted his head to the sky, "Arion," he whispered. "If you are there, please help us. Save my friends at least."

But Star's heart grew heavier. The wind and snow howled and raged, and his bones began to ache. He felt the last drops of energy ebbing away from him. Even Ella was defeated. Below her friends, she too lay down and closed her eyes.

It seemed all hope was gone. Then Star suddenly looked to the sky once more, distracted by a noise above him. It came faintly at first, like a strange screeching. Star's eyes opened in amazement as he caught sight of a large brown shape moving towards him. Its path was irregular, and now and then it was buffeted sideways by the terrible blasts of wind. Then just as it was overhead, it was suddenly caught in a scurrying loop of air. There was an ear-piercing screech, and the thing fell like a stone. It landed in a snowdrift, not three paces from where Star was standing. There was a flurry of snowflakes, and then a large brown shape began to hop and shout, as a series of angry sounds, which Star recognised clearly, exploded from its beak.

"Nevermore, nevermore. Irresponsible…"

"Migisi!" cried the amazed stallion.

The flustered eagle swung round and peered angrily at Star.

"Migisi, it is you. What are you doing here?"

"What am I doing here, well you may ask!" snapped the eagle. "Migisi hears things. A foolhardy band of horses trying to climb a mountain at the time of the snows, in a blizzard. Are you completely without sense? Didn't Nanuq tell you not to venture up the mountain in the snows? Do you think the Prophecy will protect you up here? Oh no, it won't, you will die, and then what?" Migisi stared intently at the stallion.

The stallion avoided her gaze. "But I needed to know."

The eagle rounded on Star. "This is not about you, there is much more at stake here," screeched the angry Migisi.

Star was taken aback. He had never heard his friend speak to him like this before.

"I'm sorry. I wasn't thinking," said Star, bowing his head in shame.

"No, you weren't. When you are a leader, you must take everything into consideration and not just think of yourself," replied Migisi. The eagle calmed. "Now we must get you off this ledge before we all perish."

"But how?"

"There is a way down to the cave below where your friend is. It's difficult but possible. Along there," gestured Migisi with her beak. "A thin ledge, a little jump and then a cautious horse can make it."

Star's face filled with hope.

"But you'd better hurry, or none of us will see the morning. Nevermore, nevermore. Follow me." Migisi flapped her wings and tried to take off. On the first attempt, the wind was so strong, she was almost blown back against the mountain but just managed to launch herself out over the edge, where Ella had fallen and with furious screeching disappeared into the storm.

Star rallied his friends. Bruma could hardly stand, but with Migisi circling and screeching above them the group set off. With some difficulty, they traversed the small ledge. Tarn had actually seen it earlier, but what he had been unable to see was that if they made it to its furthest point and jumped a little way to the left, they could reach a lower slope that banked less steeply.

Tarn made the first jump, then Armand and Misty. Chub slipped a little, but he made it too. Star waited behind to help his mother, and when it came to it, he was terrified that she would fall. But Bruma seemed to raise herself to the challenge, and with Migisi flapping her wings and screeching encouragement, the old mare threw herself out over the edge and landed safely with the others. Finally, Star came and soon the party found themselves edging downwards. The ground opened out, and after a little time, through the bitter wind and snow, they spotted Ella.

She led them straight along the mountainside to the cave mouth. It was a narrow opening with a boulder lip, but inside it was unexpectedly large. It was dry too and comparatively warm. Migisi joined them as an exhausted Bruma lay down by the entrance and closed her eyes.

At first, Star resisted entry, a strange sensation coming to him. Ella sensed his nervousness.

"What is it Star?"

"I don't know? Something familiar about this place...yet very strange. Man has been here, but long, long ago."

"Well we can't stay out here Star, or we'll freeze," urged Ella.

Star agreed and reluctantly entered. Migisi nestled on a ledge nearby. She fluffed up her feathers and buried her head under her wing. The exhausted horses huddled together grateful to be out of the howling night. Sleep came quickly to most of them that evening.

Ella rested by Star's side, and now she laid her head against his neck. Star felt suddenly angry and ashamed.

"I'm sorry, Ella," he murmured. "If I'd lost you I don't know what I would have done. Migisi's right, I should never have put you all in this danger."

But Ella was already asleep.

The only sound in the cave now was their breathing and the moaning wind. Star's eyes scanned the blackness around as if searching for something. Star closed his eyes and slept.

In his sleep, Star had the sense that he was coming closer to a great mystery. It had something to do with the cave and that soon another piece of that knowledge would reveal itself.

In truth, they had come to a very mysterious place. For here in this cave thousands of years before, the first humans had settled, after crossing the great land bridge to the north-west, as did the first horses.

The morning brought a welcome change in conditions. Stiff and weary, Star and his friends woke to a shaft of sunlight streaming into the cave, which immediately lifted their mood. Outside the snow had stopped temporarily and the clouds were suddenly punctured by a weak light that reached right to the back wall.

The stallion was keen to use this break in the weather to move on. He could see, however, that his friends were in no fit state, just yet, to continue the arduous climb. He sensed a change in his mother also. Her breathing was shallow, and she wheezed terribly in great pain. Star didn't wake her. He knew the best healer now was rest. He remembered what Migisi had said to him and decided not to press them to leave.

Stretching his legs, Chub had moved to the back of the cave, exploring. His eyes scanned something strange that he had not seen before.

"Come and l-l-look at this," he called.

Star and the others joined him. On the arching wall, faint but unmistakable, were the coloured images of running horses and humans. Along with these, some petroglyph etchings were scratched into the rock face, depicting a story of a bygone era thousands of years before. The sight hushed the friends. They looked at each other with their huge, startled eyes at a wall covered in various images, quite beyond their understanding.

Migisi joined them, settling next to Star.

"What is this Migisi?" said the stallion.

Migisi shook her head. She had never seen anything like this before.

Star's eyes scanned the drawings. Humans and horse, with heavy loads, a journey of some sort. A mountain range, where crops were grown. Then, the tone gradually changed. His gaze followed on to some disturbing images. The mountain spewed red, and death came. Calm was replaced by bold strokes of black and red, where men now attacked horses, killing them. Next to these killings was what looked like a tall pillar of stone, with smaller etchings on its face. Bodies of horses were piled high, and the colour red dominated the murals. Star gasped. It was just as Nanuq had told him. Horrific scenes of carnage, mutilation and what appeared to be some form of sacrifice to the mountain. Then a bright light, and humans seemed to flee, then nothing.

Once man and animal seemed to have lived in harmony, but in his attempt to control and dominate, humankind succeeded in affecting nature. The mountain appeared to hold a power and mystery that all felt.

The group looked to Star for reassurance, and though it made sense to move on while the calm prevailed, none seemed keen, and Star sensed this.

"We will rest up here until the next light. This place will give us protection until we have recovered enough to finish the climb," said Star.

The horses settled once more, glad of a chance to rest. The day progressed, and the horses slept fitfully. Weather changes were rapid in this mountainous terrain, and soon the blizzards raged about them, whistling and driving in flurries of white.

Star was the only one whose sleep eluded him. He stood at the entrance for hours at the ever-changing conditions, glancing back from time to time at the murals, troubled and fascinated by their depictions, ever eager to unlock more knowledge, to understand his purpose in life and the weight of the Prophecy that had burdened his soul.

Night came and with it an eerie calm. For the first time in many moons, the stars shone clear and bright. The young stallion stepped outside. His warm breath rose in puffs of white vapour against the icy night.

The horse looked to the sky, and suddenly a strange luminescent shimmer of emerald green sped across the blackness. This was followed shortly by a waterfall of fire and light, a swirling, whirling, spectrum of colour, rising and falling like some ghostly dancers, bright and hauntingly beautiful beyond belief. He gasped in wondered awe. This was the first time that the stallion had witnessed the magical display of the Aurora.

There, near the top of the mountain, Star stood alone, mesmerised by nature's offering. His mind began to drift as the throb of psychedelic colours held him in a state of trance. It was as though he could suddenly see for miles; there was no snow. The greens of the night sky became the greens of his home Prairies that lay before him. Herds of wild horses moved freely across them. Then images came to him from his dreams, and though he knew he wasn't asleep, they were as clear as day.

He called out to the heavens, "Arion. Where are you? I'd thought to find you here. Do you exist except in hopes, dreams or stories? Are these horses sacrificed in your name? I was always taught that you were a force for good. Why then do you allow so much pain, without action? If I am truly sent, what would you have me do to put things right?"

For a moment the stallion waited for an answer in the aching silence of the world as his vision receded, before turning, head bowed, towards the cave entrance.

He didn't notice the presence of another nearby.

"Some say these lights are the spirits of our ancestors or a fire bridge which the souls of our kind climb to be with Arion."

Star spun around, startled at first, trying to locate the voice.

In front of him, in the snow, stood a horse, not a kind that Star had seen before and certainly not a formidable towering colossus that he had imagined Arion to be if indeed this was he.

Covered almost entirely in fur, his body was short and stocky with a straight neck and short wide feet. His dun-coloured coat was dense and his black mane and tail thick and long.

At first, Star thought this was a vision before him. He stopped and blinked and then his breath failed him as he realised that this was no vision at all but as real as the mountain and the snow and the cold, cold air.

"Arion, is that you?" gasped the young stallion. "You've come at last."

Momentarily distracted by a sound coming from the cave, Star turned eagerly back to confront this strange horse. Nothing, just the moaning of the wind.

Confused and frustrated, the young stallion ran back and forth in a desperate frenzy.

"No, where have you gone!?" he shouted to the growing wind, rearing in defiance at the elements.

"Where has who gone, Star?" came a gentle sound behind him. Ella emerged from the cave to join him.

His head swirled in perplexed agony before calming. Ella saw the loss in his dark eyes.

"What is it Star. What did you see?"

The stallion stared once more into the blackness, hoping. But there was just the raging storm.

"Nothing, it was just my imagination." His shoulders sagged, and with a big sigh, he returned to the safety of the cave.

Chapter 8

Once again, the blizzard raged through the night, and the horses slept fitfully in the cave, especially Star whose encounter with the strange, mystery horse, played over and over in his mind. They heard the wind die in the middle of the next morning. Armand was the first to venture outside. The cave mouth was now completely blocked with snow, and he was forced to push and shove at the white wall to clear an opening. But when at last he had made one, the sunshine streamed through gloriously. The others began to help him, and soon they were all outside on the firm ground, enjoying the brief spell of warmth and the fresh air and thanking Arion they were still alive.

All but Star, he had stayed behind, drawn once more to the cave paintings they had all looked at earlier. The scene of bright lights over the mountain looked very similar to what he had experienced the previous night. His eyes were drawn back to the grim picture of sacrificed horses, and he wondered what it all meant. The spell was broken by the soft voice of a mare. Ella had come back to find him.

"Star, are you coming? We should try to make progress, while the weather holds."

He nodded his agreement, taking one last long look at the mural, before joining the others outside.

With Migisi soaring above them, the group began to thread their way slowly back along the path towards the spot where they had descended to the cave. Some way beyond it the ground opened again and they found that the way was easier.

It was a strange sight. High on the side of this great mountain range, moving in single file, seven horses rising up through the winter white. Like mountaineers who roped themselves together in lines, the horses followed carefully in one another's hoof marks, leaping now and then to free their legs of powder.

Armand, ever the story teller, began to imagine that they were there with the Gods and Spirits of old, climbing to the heavens to meet them. "Oh, what a story this will make when we get back home."

Home seemed such a long way away but Armand's certainty and conviction in his voice that he thought they would someday return, buoyed the rest of them.

Star lifted his head to the summit. The sky was as blue as a fresh crocus. The snow flashed and sparkled in the sunshine and crunched pleasantly underfoot. Now and then gentle gusts of wind would lift the surface around them and whirl the snow into the icy air. He kept thinking of the previous night's event and even began to question his own sanity. Did it actually happen?

It was close to the afternoon when they neared the summit and with one last steep ridge to traverse, they finally reached the top. The mountain opened broad and flat in front of them. A southerly wind was blowing, and out of excitement and relief, the horses started to race through the snow. Star looked up to see Migisi circling above his head.

"Goodbye, goodbye," screeched the eagle. "You've done it. You've climbed the mountain in the snows, just as Arion is supposed to have done. That is something to tell the world."

"Thank you, my friend, I couldn't have done it without you," called Star.

But as the eagle spoke with Star, Armand realised that he too could understand what the bird was saying.

"Remember, young stallion, this is not just about you. Be wise in your thoughts and deeds."

"Won't you stay, Migisi," whinnied Star.

"I must keep my watch over the world, but I will see you again, Star. Farewell, farewell."

The eagle circled higher and higher, riding the thermals until he became a tiny speck etched against the blue. Then he was gone.

Star ran on, his heart suddenly expectant. The others were ahead of him now, and when he came to a halt next to Ella, the horses were silent. Star's heart began to race as he followed their gaze.

The land glittered before them. Mountains and valleys, swathed in white, floating below like mighty clouds.

Chub broke the moment, gesturing to the horizon. "W-w-well we can't stay here."

Great dark snow clouds were billowing before them. The weather was changing again.

"We should get down the other side as quick as possible," said Armand.

He looked over to Star, and the stallion nodded. So with Armand leading, the horses began to descend. Only Star lingered, with Ella by his side.

"Come on, Star, we should be going," she urged.

"You go, Ella. I want to be alone for a while." He pondered a moment then whispered to himself. "Maybe he'll come if I'm alone again." He turned to Ella. "Don't worry, I'll join you soon."

Ella nodded and set off after the others. There on the top of the mountain, Star stood alone, and he felt bitterly disappointed. The stallion gazed across the rocky edges and bluffs scanning for a sign. Nothing... With a heavy heart, Star left that place and galloped off to join his friends.

Watching from a hidden vantage point was another horse. He had followed the party from the cave, always far enough behind not to be detected.

The clouds on the mountain top behind turned black and brooding as Star caught up with the others.

Star led them down the mountain into a valley just as the light began to fade. Star suggested they rest for a while. Food had been hard to find on the slopes, so each of them began to forage through the snow. As Star tried to find what food he could, his ears pricked, scanning for clues, a sound of sorts unnerved the stallion. He wandered up to where he had heard the noise and though there was no one there he could still make out the ground was scuffed away as if a horse had been watching for some time.

Star trotted back to the group. Chub noticed a look of concern on his friend's face.

"W-w-what is it Star?"

"We're being watched I think."

Chub immediately stiffened his stance.

"Stay alert, but don't mention anything to the others yet until I'm sure."

Chub nodded, his eyes now wide and alert.

Chub and Star took turns to watch over their friends that evening and were glad to see the sun rise once more without incident.

The following morning the horses ventured further up the valley, and soon even the others began to pick up a familiar scent. Almost immediately they saw four horses coming towards them. They were all females, but when they reached the friends, they completely ignored the stallions, and the leading mare went straight up to Ella.

"May Arion be with you," she said curtly.

Ella was quite confused by this strange greeting.

"And with you," said Ella coldly.

"Where have you come from?" said the mare.

Ella had taken an instant dislike to this horse. She felt like turning and giving her a kick with her hoof. Tarn came forward, but Star stepped in his way and nodded to Ella.

"From the south," answered Ella.

"Hmmm. That's well," said the mare. "For a while, we thought your stallions were…"

She paused.

"But it would be too soon for the Collection," she went on.

Star immediately understood. His mind raced to his time with Nanuq. "Maidens," he whispered to himself.

"Where are the other mares?" continued the lead female.

"There are no others mares," answered Ella, "except me, Misty and Bruma."

"So you lead the Band?"

Ella looked to Star, who nodded very gently again. "Yes."

"Good," said the mare. My name is Felise.

Ella hardly cared to answer, but she decided on tact.

"Mine is Ella. This is Star. He…"

"This is Jetta, Kiowa and Lita," said Felise, interrupting Ella and still ignoring the stallions. "If you come with us we shall show you to our Band. You are welcome enough, I suppose. At least our stallions could do with some help."

"That's very kind of you, I'm sure, said Ella sharply, holding back the anger, "but I must ask my friends. Star has been very…"

"Do you lead or not?" snapped Felise. "Perhaps you've been too long alone. Bring the stallions, and we will put them with the others."

Felise turned away disdainfully, leaving the amazed party alone again.

"What cheek," said Ella. I'd like to bite her."

"It's very strange," agreed Star. "Nanuq told me that through them we would find the Guardians, so let us go along with this for now."

So the party followed, with Ella, Bruma and Misty taking the lead. The rest of what was a Band, of some fifty horses, was grazing further up the valley, around the banks of a river. It looked a safe enough spot, and there were good vantage points to spy for any predators. The closer Star got he noticed that it was just as Nanuq had told him, that they were nearly all females.

The main body was bunched by the waterside drinking or grazing and as the group approached some looked at the stallions coldly or turned their backs on them. Felise was waiting for them, and she addressed Star for the first time.

"You," she said. "You'll find the stallions over there." Ask for Nacho. He'll tell you what to do."

Star's temper was beginning to fray, but he decided to bide his time. So, with only a wink to Ella, he led the stallions off up the hill.

The main party of males was a way off. There were around fifteen stallions. Star and the others trotted up to them.

"I'm looking for a stallion by the name of Nacho," he said.

The horse blinked but said nothing and instead pointed vaguely with his head. Nacho was higher up still, chewing on some vegetation that he had uncovered beneath the snow.

"Why are the mares in charge?" said Tarn

"It's always been that way here," answered Nacho. "We do what we're told, and they look after us."

"Look after you?" snorted Tarn with disgust.

"Yes, but mostly we keep separate until we're needed for mating. Then the mares come and choose some among us. So the herd goes on serving the Guardians."

"The mares choose you?" gasped Armand. They were all amazed now.

"Yes," replied Nacho, as though it was the most natural thing in the world.

"That's not natural," responded Tarn.

Nacho munched on a soft spray of vegetation and then shrugged with no apparent interest in finding out anything from the newcomers of their life.

"What can you tell me of the Guardians, Nacho," said Star.

"They are to the west, beyond the Worship Stone. That's all I know."

Star pawed the ground. "What is the Worship Stone?"

"This is where they come together to honour Arion," said Nacho.

"We need to find them."

"That is forbidden. It would be sacrilege."

Although desperate to ask many more questions, Star thought it best not to rush things.

When Star and the others had left the mares, Ella and Misty had found a comfortable spot for Bruma to rest and set to work finding out as much as they could about this strange herd. They all looked healthy. Several of them had foals, and these mares seemed to enjoy a particular position in the Band, for the stallions would bring the mothers food, especially those mothers suckling colts.

Ella and Misty mingled with the other mares and met with Lita, one of the horses that she first encountered at the river with Felise.

"You don't think much of the stallions, do you?" said Misty.

Lita munched on thoughtfully before lifting her gaze to Misty. "There's not much to think of really. We all do our duty to serve Arion."

"Tell me," said Ella. "Do you not miss the companionship?"

Lita was thoughtful again. "It's been six seasons now."

"So long? And you never wanted to be with anyone?" queried Ella.

"No," said Lita, almost sadly.

"But why?" asked Misty.

"There are plenty of mares here who often are with a stallion. If they're lucky, they will have beautiful daughters and watch them grow. But there's always a chance that... you know..."

"No," said Misty "What?"

"I had two beautiful colts."

"And?" pressed Ella.

"I couldn't face it again. But that's what happens if you have one. They might be chosen, and they're really very sweet when they're so young. You get to miss them."

Ella looked gravely at her sister.

"So they only take the colts?" asked Ella.

"Of course."

"And they chose both yours?" said Misty quietly.

Lita nodded, and though her face had grown a little sad again, there was a strange confusion in her eyes.

"Do you know what happens to them?" said Ella kindly.

"No one really knows," answered Lita, and her face brightened. "But Felise says they are honoured, and when He comes, they will take their rightful place by His side and heal the lands once more."

As Ella and Misty walked back towards Bruma, they pondered their discussion with Lita.

It was the following evening, and a new moon had come up. Star and the others were grazing when Chub lifted his head. A horse was coming downwind towards them, and through the darkness, they saw Ella. She looked grave and was obviously doing her best to remain concealed.

"I've found you," she whispered as she came up. "I had to skirt around the valley to avoid being seen."

"What's wrong, Ella?" said Star.

"Nothing. But they don't like the mares talking to the stallions. They say it's unnatural."

"What have you found out?" he asked.

"There must be almost one hundred horses in the valley, and the mares tend to congregate at a place called the gathering ground. This is where everything is brought for the 'Collection'."

"When they take the foals?"

"Yes," said Ella gravely. "And they only take the colts, it seems. It's part of an ancient ritual. They say they are waiting for The One to come."

"Did you find out anything about these Guardians?"

Ella shook her head. "I didn't want to make anyone suspicious by asking too many questions."

"I'm not sure there's much point asking them." Nacho said, "it is forbidden to know. The only thing we can do is to lay low and wait until the great thaw when they come again for the Collection, then somehow we can try to follow them. In the meantime, it will give us a chance to learn a little more about them. Perhaps make some friends here too. We may have need of them in the future if we ever want to rid our lands of Shade."

Ella nodded.

"How is my mother?"

"The rest here will do her good, and she is being well cared for." She smiled briefly and nuzzled her head into his.

"I miss you," she said fondly. "I better get back to Misty and Bruma. We'll try and come and see you when we can."

"Good," said Star.

"And Star," said Ella, smiling as she turned to leave, "try not to work too hard."

So, as the cold season settled around them they stayed with the Maidens, and though Bruma was little help, Ella and Misty devoted themselves to winning over some of the mares, while the others made friends among the few stallions.

Chapter 9

"Alive? What do you mean alive?"

Caius backed away nervously into the shadows. He had never seen Shade so angry. His master was older now, and hairs around his muzzle were flecked with grey, which somehow gave a more sinister aspect to the scar across his face.

"But how?" said Shade in disbelief.

"Our scouts caught a young horse who swears it was Star. From what they found out, he was rescued," said Caius his voice dropping away to a frightened whisper, "by humans."

"By humans?" whispered Shade. For the first time, Caius noticed something like fear flicker across Shade's single eye. But it soon passed.

"Where did they find this informer?"

"To the far north-west of here, near the great mountains."

Shade let out a sudden gasp. Once again Caius detected concern in his master's tone. "And?"

"He said something else… This Star was seeking answers to something and was going to cross the mountain to find the Guardians?"

Shade swung round suddenly and glared at Caius.

"Yes," he said.

"You know them, my lord?" said Caius with surprise.

"A little," replied Shade. "Go on."

"That was it, my lord."

Shade's body visibly shuddered, and he twisted his form away from Caius. "He will find them and our secrets. He will unite everyone. He will not deny me my revenge," he whispered to himself.

"He has also joined up with the three stallions and mares that our Zellats were after, my lord."

Shade quickly regained his composure and spun back to face Caius.

"Bring me this horse."

Caius lowered his head.

"He got away."

"Am I surrounded by incompetents?" cried Shade.

"Take me to the scouts Caius, quickly. I will have words with them myself."

Caius led Shade to the scouts, who were waiting fearfully for their leader, surrounded by a contingent of Zellat bodyguards.

"You," cried Shade, as he ran up to one of them and thrust his muzzle straight into the horse's terrified face, "tell me everything you know about Star and what you heard and saw. Leave nothing out. I warn you, I'll know if you're embellishing it just to please me."

So the stallion began. He spoke falteringly at first until Shade shouted at him and threatened him, so he went on, describing the chase up the mountain until the weather became so severe that they lost him. He also mentioned a weird light that shone over the mountain one night, which seemed to capture Shade's thought. Shade pondered the story.

"My lord," said the Zellat scout suddenly, "can this Prophecy be real?"

The stallion regretted the question immediately. Shade attacked, burying his teeth into the horse's throat. The scout struggled furiously, and when Shade finally let go, blood was gushing from his neck.

"You know it is death to talk of the Prophecy," cried Shade.

He spun around and addressed the small group of Zellats.

"All of you," he cried, "listen carefully to me. Not a word of what you have heard tonight must pass your lips. Do you understand me? Not a single word. As far as you're concerned this… Star, died. It will be hard on you if I find that any of it has leaked out to the herds. Do you understand?"

The scouts and the assembled Zellat bodyguards nodded.

"Very well then," he said, his tone becoming soft and conciliating as he turned to the scouts. "You have done well, and I am pleased. We will find an honoured place for your loyal service."

Much to the relief of the gathered stallions Shade left with Caius.

But as he ran his eye was burning brightly.

"Caius," said Shade quietly when they were some distance away. "I want them disposed of."

"My lord?"

"Get rid of them, Caius. It's the only way to be sure."

"The scouts my lord?" said Caius.

"No, Caius, you idiot, not just the scouts. All of them. But try to do it subtly, Caius. Arrange some accidents. Pick them off one by one."

Caius ventured a question. He knew that he was the only stallion in the Valley who could have got away with it.

"My lord," he said softly.

"What is it, Caius?"

"The Prophecy,"

"What about it?" said Shade irritably, but he seemed strangely distracted.

"Can it be coming true? We know he can speak to other animals, one who could speak with many tongues…"

"Yes Caius, I know the words to the Prophecy," said Shade abruptly. "It is a surprise, I admit," continued Shade coldly, "to hear he has survived, nothing more."

"But he has spent time with man."

Shade was silent now, for somewhere in his own black heart doubt and fear began to flutter and linger.

"No," cried Shade, his spirit suddenly rallying, "all we have to fear from Star is the superstition and stupidity of horses. That's why all that were witness to this story tonight must be silenced. I do not believe in this Prophecy, but I know that belief is a very powerful force, whether the object of that belief is true or not. But there is something else that can only work in our favour. These scouts of ours said that Star had met up with the others, so it means that Bruma is with him, which can only mean that he himself does not believe yet. He does not know that he is Abrazo and Gaia's colt, which gives us time to organise and to have this Star removed before others rally to his cause, before he can convince himself and others that there is something in this story."

Shade looked intently to Caius. "It is time I met this Star. Send out the Zellats and summon all the

Bands to me. I will take the great herd north and crush him once and for all. The Prophecy will not protect him against my vast army. Now go."

Shade watched Caius gallop away. "And you my Guardians of Arion, I will have my revenge," he whispered to himself through grinding teeth.

Several moons had passed, and the great herd began to mass on the Prairie. Those who had pledged their alliance to Shade had come, all but one.

Caius approached his leader. "Your army is almost assembled, my lord. Only Morro has declined your invitation."

"Morro. We will deal with him, in good time," said Shade.

He cast his eye across his harem and his gaze settled on Gaia. She was old now, like Shade, but his heart still stirred at how beautiful she still looked. Since the day of Zell's death Shade had kept her by his side, hoping against hope that perhaps, one day, she might grow to love him. She would never pair with him, he knew that, but she was his prize, and he would never let her go. Abrazo's love, the boldest and most beautiful of all the Prairie mares.

He realised of course that it was only his threat of doing harm to Rosa and Aiko that held her. For after the news he had given her at the ravine, Gaia hardly cared whether she lived or died and it was only the thought of protecting them that kept her from doing herself some fatal harm.

If only you knew that your son Star was alive, thought Shade now as he looked at her. That might bring back the spark to your eyes. But, Gaia, my dear, you must never know.

The morning had broken like shattered stone around the grazing herd. The icy sky was as white and bleak as loss itself. A heavy frost blanketed the ground and what grass that could be seen seemed to have been drained of colour. Shade's breath hung like a wraith around his lips as he stared out across the Prairie and as the light came, his heart swelled at the sight that met his eye. The impressive ranks of his fanatical Zellats ranged across the Plains along with those that had come to pay homage to him. With every sun, more came to add to Shade's might.

They were his children now, and Shade gave a deep sigh of satisfaction. Gaia stirred and looked bitterly across at Shade.

He ambled towards her, "good morning my dear."

Gaia ignored him.

"There is much to do this sun, Gaia," said Shade, "and I would like you to accompany me as I address my family."

"They are not your family, Shade. It is only their fear that brings them here. I will not stand with you," whispered Gaia coldly.

"Come, come, Gaia, you must learn to be more civil," said Shade. "Otherwise, perhaps I shall ask Rosa and Aiko to join me instead."

Gaia, glared at him, before nodding her head wearily, obediently. She had heard the threat a hundred times, and now she was simply too tired to resist. There was nothing left for the poor mare to resist with.

"Very well, Shade," she said quietly.

Caius led Shade and Gaia forward to the edge of the hill, where an earth mound gave them a perfect vantage across the Prairie and the best position from which to address the herd.

Caius stepped forward. The horses below them were already hushed for they had been told to expect some words from their leader.

Shade stepped forward, and as he did so, a great rumble went up. It started at the back and swept forward like a wave rushing to meet the shore.

"SHADE!" came the thunderous cry. "SHADE!"

The sound crashed over their leader, and he felt himself swell in stature as the power of their voices moved through him like blood turned into pure energy. He paused, basking in the glory of it all, as the sea subsided and became a ripple of awed whispering.

"Silence," cried Shade and the stillness was immediate.

"Welcome, my friends," he began. "Your loyalty touches me. Our strength has grown. I have given you all this. Not some mythical spirit or god. Me! I have forged these alliances and made us powerful. No longer do we need to trust in dreams and hope. We deal in reality. Guided by my will, we will take what we want and destroy anyone that stands in our way. Faith is a sign of weakness. It is time that we cleansed all the lands of this superstitious nonsense." Shade stared intently at the gathering. "Do you embrace the cult of death."

"Yes we embrace it!" came the frenzied shout, prompted by his fanatical Zellats.

"I will lead you north to victory, and anyone who opposes us will die by our hooves. No longer will the words Arion be spoken in these lands. The name of Arion will die with the last of his kind!"

Another volley of noise rang out, provoked once more by his Zellats.

"ARION IS DEAD TO US! LONG LIVE SHADE! ARION IS DEAD TO US! LONG LIVE SHADE!"

Shade smiled grimly as he turned to Gaia. "So my dear, soon I will finish those few in the north that oppose my will and Arion will be no more."

"You're mad, Shade," whispered Gaia.

"No, my dear, I am quite sane. For only sanity and reason could have seen the dawn of this brave day."

"I hate you Shade for what you have done to our kind. I will hate you until the stars grow cold."

Shade felt a tightening in his gut. He wanted to hurt Gaia then. But he held his urge in check, for his knowledge that her beloved Star was still alive, without her even knowing it, gave him a strange power over her.

"Well, my dear," he said, almost indifferently, "then we shall have to come up with something even better to please you, won't we? But rest assured, soon I will be Lord of all, not just the wild horses but all animals will bow before my might."

His eye fired with a burning madness that sent a chill down Gaia's spine.

*****

To the north, a single Mustang was gazing down from the forest at the shining spring waters. He was lost in thought and twisted with the guilt that had given him this privilege of Leader of his Band.

The other stallions stirred restlessly, for they knew that Shade was on the move and that if it came to it, flight would be their best hope.

Their leader shook his head. Morro had grown into a strong and powerful horse. His eyes were unsettled, and sadness cloaked his spirit. He had regretted to this day his dark deed and alliance with Shade to rid this Band of Leonardo. Why hadn't he just fought him, he thought to himself bitterly? He could have beaten him in a fair fight. But Shade's Zellats and Caius had come to him, whispering of certainty and promising alliances and his greed and ambition, allowed darkness to envelop his thoughts.

"That's why I did it," Morro told himself now, "to help preserve things. Shade would have just taken everything." But he knew that it was only half true. Morro was only too aware of the heights, or depths, of his own ambition.

"Leonardo was a fool," he told himself half-heartedly, trying to summon thoughts to console himself. "He should have hidden his belief in Arion. I was practical. Look where principal got him. Now he is dead. Besides, I was the strongest," said Morro quietly. "I was the best, so it was only right that I took over the herd."

So why had it hurt all this time? Again, confusion entered his mind. Morro had Leonardo's blood on him, and not even the rushing mountain rivers could wash that guilt away.

So instead of his heart swelling with pride all these seasons as the Leader of his Band, he felt a terrible remorse.

And what had he done it all for? To see Shade eventually take everything anyway? It was not homage that Shade wanted but total dominion, and he would stop at nothing until all bowed to his way.

"What a fool I've been," said Morro to himself bitterly, as he looked to the sky. "Forgive me, Leonardo."

Morro's troubled thoughts were suddenly interrupted by the approach of six stallions from his Band. They were led by Blake, the horse who had first welcomed Bruma, Star, and the others those years before. Blake, like the others, had been running hard and he looked almost exhausted.

Morro turned to face them. "Blake. What news?"

Blake looked grave.

"Bad news, my lord. They are less than two suns from here, though they seem to have stopped for a while."

"How many?" asked Morro.

"It's hard to tell," answered Blake, shaking his head. "The herd stretched as far as the eye could see, maybe two thousand or more graze across the Prairie. The dust cloud almost blotted out the sun."

Morro's eyes opened wide at the sheer scale of this. He pondered a moment then looked at his Band.

"Then the time has come," said Morro quietly.

"What shall we do, Lord Morro?" asked Blake.

Morro looked at Blake. "You who have served me despite what I did to Leonardo. You tell me what I should do."

"There are rumours my lord."

"Rumours?"

"Yes, my lord. There have been for some time. There is talk of the Prophecy once more. Some say that Star did not die as was first thought. That he lives in the north."

Morro said nothing for a while as he gazed across the valley. He had hated Star, but now this strange news came like a breath of hope from some distant place, carried on the wind to a land where all hope had gone.

"Shall we take the Band north my lord and find him?"

Morro was still silent.

"If others have rallied to his cause, we could make a stand there."

"I will not abandon my home for anyone," said Morro suddenly.

"But my lord, they are far too strong for us."

Morro looked to Blake. "Lead the Band north, find this stallion. Hopefully, the rumours are true. Save our kind and help build a force to defeat Shade."

"But lord," replied Blake.

"Go now, while there is still time. I have lived with this guilt for too long. I must now do the right thing."

"But you will surely perish. A pointless waste," said Blake.

"Not pointless, Blake. For I plan to win you time. And who knows, if I can get close enough to Shade…"

Blake bowed, a mutual understanding passing between the two.

Blake gathered all the mares, stallions, foals and colts together, and later that morning led them away from the valley that had been their home for generations, their hearts resigned to the long trek north to their hopeful safety.

Morro remained in the eerie silence that now pervaded the place, awaiting his fate, but somehow calmed by the years of guilt that had now left him.

When they came, it was not like the storm he was expecting. The sun shone brightly on the calm green land as ten Zellats sauntered into the valley.

Caius, who led them, smiled coldly as he spotted Morro. Shade's commander led the Zellats to their quarry.

"Lord Morro," said Caius, without bowing, "Lord Shade is waiting for you."

"Waiting for what?" snorted Morro.

"For you to renew your oath of homage to him," answered Caius.

Morro looked into Caius' eyes, and Caius held his gaze openly and in a knowing slightly amused way. At that moment Morro saw his own fate He did not resist, he was almost glad, now that it had come.

"Very well," he said quietly. I will accompany you."

Without another word, Morro sped off, led away by Caius and the Zellats.

It took Caius a couple of suns to reach Shade, and when Morro finally saw the size of the herd, he trembled at the sight. Shade was set apart, on a hill and though he was encircled by his guards, they had been ordered to stand as far apart from him as they could while making sure of his safety.

Caius led Morro forward through the ring of Zellats.

"So you've come, Morro," said Shade casually. "Are you ready to renew your homage?"

"If need be," said Morro coldly.

Shade smiled. "Well, it's about this pact of ours I wanted to talk about. I'm rather bored with it. There is no place for another lord, don't you see?"

If Shade had expected the news to startle Morro he was disappointed, for the stallion looked back at him without emotion.

"Do you think I'm such a fool," said Morro quietly, "to believe that our pact meant anything?"

"Then why are you here?" said Shade.

Morro didn't answer, but Shade looked at him his eye suddenly glittered.

"I see," he said, "how noble. You thought to buy your Band time, didn't you Morro? Time to escape?"

Morro dropped his eyes.

"My poor Morro," whispered Shade. "If you think you've helped them I'm afraid you're mistaken. Even before Caius arrived at your valley, I'd already sent my

Zellats to skirt north of your position. So as we speak, your little 'family' are being destroyed."

Morro looked up and stared at Shade in horror, but he knew immediately that Shade was telling the truth. Morro's heart filled with fury, and he reared up at Shade. But as he did so Caius thrust himself forward and knocked Morro off balance. In an instance, the Zellats surrounded their leader.

"Bravely done, Morro," said Shade contemptuously from behind the wall of bodyguards, "but you shall pay for that."

Morro recovered himself and raised his head to Shade. "Very well," he said quietly. "Get on with it."

"Get on with what?"

"You brought me here to kill me, Shade," said Morro quietly. "The sacrifice will have been in vain, but I no longer care to live."

"The sacrifice?" said Shade. "How touching. I have no intention of killing you right now, Morro. I will have the Zellats amuse themselves with you, and then you will be forced to live your painful life with the herd as their pleasure. My gift to them, so to speak."

The Zellats drove him away. Shade stood and watched this broken stallion leave and Shade was pleased.

Shade turned to his commander. "Caius, is he ready?"

"Yes, lord, he is waiting nearby."

"Then bring him to me."

Caius nodded and ran down the slope. When he returned, there was a young stallion with him. There was a cold, ruthless look in his eyes.

"You have your orders," said Shade as they arrived.

The young stallion nodded silently.

"We must put an end to these lies and rumours, once and for all," said Shade, "so there must be no mistake, no mistake at all."

Again the stallion nodded and then he turned silently and galloped away. His purpose carried a foreboding grimness, a purpose for which he had been specially trained and made ready for this very moment. A mission that lay far to the north.

156

Chapter 10

The weather had grown milder as the season progressed and the snows were already beginning to melt. Star had seen less and less of Misty and Ella and spent his time with the other stallions, Chub, Armand and Tarn, foraging as was required of them.

The dishevelled grasses soon became lush, erasing even the memory of their wintry selves. The trees budded with leaf and blossom, and the harsh sleet became soft rain. The rivers swelled with melt water, and the only thick blanket of brilliant white remained on the peaks of the mountains that ringed the valley.

Then the day came, Star looked across the river in the fading evening light, when he saw Misty galloping straight towards him, making no attempt to stay concealed.

"Star! She cried, as she reached him. "They've come."

"When?"

"Just now, twenty stallions arrived at the gathering place. Felice greeted them, they took the young colts and disappeared over the far ridge. Ella has followed their tracks. We need to hurry Star. I've left Bruma waiting."

"Then we must be quick," said Star, nodding to his friends.

With Star leading, the five horses sped towards Bruma. The mare was deeply bewildered when they got to her, but Misty took charge, and they made their way to the ridge where Ella was waiting for them. But as they crested the hill they pulled up.

A line of horses barred their way. Felise stood in front of the mares, and her eyes were blazing.

"What are you doing?" she cried furiously.

"We are leaving," said Star.

"I wasn't talking to you," said Felise.

"Nevertheless, I want-"

"Silence!" squealed Felise. "A stallion must not talk to the Maidens of Arion like this. Ella, where do you think you are going?"

Ella stepped forward with force.

"Get out of my way," she whispered furiously, lifting her head towards Felise.

"What?"

"I said, get out of my way."

Felise hesitated. She was not used to being talked to like this by anyone, but there was something dangerous in Ella's look that made her pause.

"We're going to follow them," said Ella.

Lita's eyes opened in amazement. "No," she gasped. "It's forbidden."

"Nevertheless." replied Ella, pressing forward aggressively barging and jostling the mare, "we are going."

Before the other horses could come to her aid Star, Tarn, Armand, Chub and Misty moved forward, isolating their leader from the pack.

Felise nodded to the mares, and they parted, allowing the group to continue. With one last stare, Ella turned and galloped over the ridge closely followed by her friends.

Star came alongside her. "That's a lesson for me to never to get into an argument with you." The stallion beamed with pride for his friend as they galloped onwards.

Star took to the front and led them on as fast as he could. Although the tracks left behind by the stallions were easy to follow in the soft ground, it soon became apparent that they were travelling at tremendous speed. After a time, the small party found it impossible to keep up. It was hard to follow their tracks over rocky terrain, but Star managed to pick up their signs in broken twigs and clumps of hair caught on the rough vegetation, or merely in the lie of the land and the most likely path a horse would follow.

Oddly, every now and then and at regular intervals, the horses came across circles left by the stallion's hooves, where they had evidently stopped to talk and scuffed the ground away. In the centre, they found broken branches or clumps of flowers or some token that seemed to have been arranged there as part of a strange rite.

When they had been travelling for four suns, the friends grew increasingly nervous. Star was especially on edge, for they grew closer to Arion's herd. Star could sense it, and his nervousness spread to them all. Anxiety filled their hearts at the thought of what might face them all. They had come this far to find answers and help to free them from the evil Shade had inflicted on their world, but the conflicting stories they had heard, brought doubt to them all, that maybe an even greater danger lurked here.

Star had little idea what he would say when they did eventually find them and was haunted by the thought of what he might discover about himself. Whenever he closed his eyes to sleep now, he dreamt of Arion.

One such dream, which came as the dawn began to chase the stars from the sky, had a profound effect on him.

In his dreams, Star found himself on a barren Prairie, and the wind was blowing around his head. The land was bleak and grey. There was a voice in the wind and Star knew that it was Arion.

"What are you seeking?" whispered the wind.

Star stirred in his sleep.

"To understand," Star found himself saying, "to be free."

"To you is granted much understanding," came the voice, "but you may not understand all things."

"Then how can I be free?"

"What is freedom," laughed the wind.

"Freedom is running with my Band," murmured Star. "Freedom is living the Mustang way."

"Yes, but what of them? The ones you left behind. Those you abandoned?"

The wind grew stronger and mixed in its cries Star heard the anguished calls of a stricken horse.

"Oh, Arion," moaned Star, as though in pain, "will you never leave me be? Will I never be free?"

"Freedom is first within," boomed the howling voice.

"But what must I do?"

"Remember what I told you long ago. You must listen, Star. Listen to what you are and never forget."

In Star's dream, the wind died to a faint echo, and all that was left was a whispering sigh on the breeze.

"You cannot run from your destiny, however hard you try. You must embrace it," said the wind and the voice and the dream were gone.

It was late morning, and the mist hung lightly across the land they were travelling over. The ground had begun to rise once more, and they all felt strangely expectant. They were cresting a ridge when Chub, who was a little way ahead, suddenly stopped.

"L-l-look," he gasped.

Ahead of them, was a large totem pillar that rose up to the height of a young tree, through the mist that curled and wisped around its sides that were hewn roughly from mountain stone by hands long dead. The surface was covered in strange scratchings, symbols and drawings similar to those they had seen in the cave.

Star remembered the cave painting, the vivid death of many horses the splashes of red, stained on the walls. He gazed at the column and wondered what horrors had beset this place. The others felt it and were sickened by it.

"W-w-what made this? stuttered Chub.

"Man."

Star was right, for the stone totem dated back tens of thousands of years, erected by the first people and it served them as a symbol to their sacred spirit. For those people, this had once been a holy place; a place to worship not the images of man or even the animals, but the raw, unconscious power of life itself: a kind of anchor to the spinning stars. As they had seen in the cave murals, great scenes of horrors had taken place here, and these atrocities echoed through the stirring energy of the site. The horses felt it now, as Star moved closer still. Their senses quivered with the touch of the unknown and the unknowable.

Star scented the earth where the ground was badly scuffed. He nodded, realising that the other party had passed by this way and only very recently.

"S-s-stay close to me, Misty," whispered Chub.

"Star, come and look at this," called Armand suddenly.

He was standing close to the stone. Near the base of the pillar, Star saw the bleached remains of a horse's skull.

"What does it mean?" whispered Armand.

Star shook his head but remembered his conversations with Nanuq and the grim possibilities of what could lurk in this place. It would appear that his worst fears were being realised. Behind him, he sensed that the others were dangerously nervous. Bruma was shaking almost uncontrollably.

"Come on," he cried, "we should keep moving."

As they followed the incline of the land, they saw ever increasing evidence of horse activity, signs of a larger group in the territory. The soft scented Prairie breeze and beauty of the day, however, eased their sense of foreboding. As the sun dropped beyond the horizon, threads of gold lingered in the sky, patterning the rolling clouds orange then red and purple as the dying light faded to a dark blue, until all that was left of the sunset was a chalky mauve. Despite the possible danger, there was a great stillness about the place.

Across the next hill, Star spotted them, grazing in the evening light. The herd was large, and it soon became evident to them that there were no mares at all.

Armand turned to Star. "What do we do now?"

"I think I should go in on my own. Then if they are hostile, you can get away."

"If you're going in, said Ella, "then we'll go in with you."

As she said that, fifteen stallions had come up behind them and were racing towards them. Instinctively, the friends turned and fled along the ridge, but now they were in full view of the rest of the herd. Stallions began to rush at them from all directions. If they had wondered whether these Guardians would be hostile, now they were left in little doubt.

"Hurry," cried Star, trying desperately to think of what to do. "Form a circle."

The small party drew together in a circle, and there they stood, in the surrounding darkness, waiting for their fate.

The stallions took no time to reach them and as they approached there was fury in their eyes. The groups came together and swept round and round the friends, stamping their hooves as they went, rearing up to paw the air.

Quite suddenly they came to a stop with the largest of the stallions facing Star.

"Get ready," Star whispered.

The lead stallion stared at Star and then stepped to one side, creating a gap in the circle and through it sauntered a small, aged, wise looking horse. Star gasped, his eyes widened in recognition. It was the same horse he had seen on the mountain that night in the storm.

There was a silence between them, and Star turned to his friends.

"Leave."

"What do you mean leave?" cried the agitated Ella.

"Go," said Star.

"No! We're not leaving you. I'm not leaving you again," pleaded Ella.

"You must," said Star. "You must go. It's me they want."

Ella looked longingly into her companion's eyes, then, slowly her stance softened.

Another gap opened up in the circle to allow the others to leave. Reluctantly and anxiously, Chub, Tarn,

Armand, Bruma, Ella and Misty vacated the ring of stallions, heads lowered.

No sooner had they done so, the circle closed behind, and the large party of stallions moved as one down the valley, with Star somewhere in the middle, leaving his abandoned friends in a state of confused despair at the top of the ridge.

Darkness shrouded the valley and the friends found shelter in a nearby copse of trees out of site, and waited for daybreak.

Morning came and the first slither of sun peeked over the skyline in a radiant white form, contrasting starkly against the grasslands which were dull in comparison.

Chub was the first to rise, and to his horror, he stared out over an empty valley.

"Ella!" he shouted, "c-c-come here, quickly."

Chub was joined one by one, by the friends. For a long moment, no one spoke.

"Where have they all gone?" said Armand.

Then fear gripped Ella, panic welled up in her face. Misty picked up on Ella's anxiety.

"What is it, Ella?"

"I know where they've gone," she said, her face ashen with fear. "They've taken Star to the Stone," then, without warning, she galloped away.

Simultaneously, images of the sacrificial cave painting came to each of them.

"Do you think they're going to kill him?" said Tarn.

"But if they believe he's the fulfiller of the Prophecy, the son of Arion, then why would they kill him?" questioned Armand.

"But what if they don't? Do we even believe?" replied Tarn.

"I-i-it could be too late already," added Chub.

Armand, Chub and Tarn sped after Ella, with Misty and Bruma close behind.

It didn't take long for them to pick up the trail and Ella was right in her assumption, the whole herd was heading to the standing stone.

By the middle of the day, Ella and the others reached a vantage point a safe distance from the Stone. To their relief, they spotted Star in the distance surrounded by a cordon of stallions that moved with him wherever he roamed among the large herd.

Armand turned to Ella, "How are we going to get through all of that?"

Ella pondered a moment. "We'll have to wait until dark, then, somehow try to rescue him."

"Even if we do, by some miracle, manage to get near to him, how do we even know he wants to be rescued? After all, he wanted to find these Guardians. And besides, he knew what the danger could be," argued an outraged Tarn.

Ella shot him a withering glare.

"What?" Tarn replied. "I came here, just like all of you, thinking we were somehow going to find help to fight against Shade and take back our homelands. Now it seems these Guardians, could be just as bad as him. What's it all been for, eh?"

None had an answer.

"Besides, do any of you actually believe in this Prophecy anyway?" he added. There was a pause as Tarn stared at each and every one of them.

"But I believe in, Star," came the defiant reply from Ella.

The other friends nodded their agreement.

Tarn understood that trying to persuade them otherwise was a waste of time.

"Fine then, you go to your death. I'm going to find other horses who'll help me fight Shade. I'm tired of running."

Tarn turned to his lifelong friend Armand. "I'm sorry Armand," and without another word galloped away.

The friends were stunned by Tarn's outburst and abandonment. Armand was visibly distressed, and Ella nuzzled him, trying to ease his pain.

Armand gazed at her blankly, "what shall we do now?" his eyes searching for some reassurance.

"We carry on with our plan," answered Ella defiantly.

Chapter 11

All day, they had discussed how best to get to Star, and by nightfall they were ready. They were all desperately nervous, but each, apart from Bruma, had their part to play and that at least helped stop them from succumbing to fear.

A warm breeze picked up, whispering through the grass. A fat, full moon rose in the sky and the ancient Stone column, a tall tree in diameter, was silhouetted against the giant yellow orb which hung like a mighty island in the ghostly sky. They could see everything in its sallow light as the wind grew stronger and stronger. The herd was gathering around the monolith. Rings of stallions circled the totem, an air of expectancy all around. In the very centre, was a form they instantly recognised. It was Star. With him, was the diminutive figure of the small horse who appeared to be leading the ceremony.

They crept nearer, hardly daring to breathe. The circles of stallions began to sway rhythmically as a voice cried out.

"Arion, Great Spirit, enlighten us. Fulfil the ancient destiny of our kind."

The wind gusted and whipped about them, and suddenly they gasped in awe as their eyes were drawn to the sky. A myriad of greens and blues, then pinks and deeper purples shimmered and stretched, across the heavens, swaying and illuminating the world in a hypnotic psychedelic display of colour. The wonderous northern lights.

Almost oblivious to nature's spectacle above, the voice continued unperturbed.

"Hail Arion, accept the offering we bring as a sign of our devotion to you. Bring the colts."

The kaleidoscope of magic lights flashed and danced above them as four stallions stepped out of the cordon and to Chub and Armand's amazement, a group of colts appeared at the far side of the circle. They walked forward slowly, swaying their heads.

"Let them dance," came the voice.

Now the stallions began to chant in unison, and the voice cried out once more as the wind picked up in intensity.

"You, who are the future, dance for Arion, dance for him now."

The colts began to sway around Star, moving in a circle and throwing their heads left and right as they went. The stallions' wailing climbed to a kind of pounding, rhythmic beat as the colts spun around and swayed under the moon. Faster and faster they went, and they seemed to turn to shadows in the ghostly night.

"Arion," cried the gathered stallions as the colts danced, "Arion, hear our cry."

The colts seemed not of this world driven by some unheard, unearthly music. The dancing rose to a fever pitch, and then, suddenly one of the colts broke from the ring and stepped up to the stone monolith. Then four stallions rushed into the centre to join the youngling.

The view became obscured as the horses moved and swayed blocking any clear sight that the friends had of Star within the circle.

"What's happening?" cried Ella frantically. "I can't see anything."

Then suddenly, they saw the stallions rise up on their haunches now visible above the jostling crowd, repeatedly bring their hooves down on the ground.

Armand turned to the friends, "I can't see clearly, but I think they're killing the colts."

"We must try to save them. Where is Star?" cried Ella.

"Not without me, you're not," came a cry from the darkness. Armand and the others turned to see Tarn.

"You came back!" said Armand.

"You're my friends, my family," Tarn replied directly.

There was a moment's pause before Ella rallied them.

"Come on!"

The brave mare leapt from her place of cover and charged her way through the ranks of stallions without a thought for her safety. Armand, Tarn, Bruma, Misty and Chub followed behind, cutting a swathe through the confused horses.

They barged their way into the sacred circle, and all eyes fell on them. The chanting subsided to a still calm.

Then the deafening silence was shattered.

"You have no business here! It is forbidden." cried the small old stallion. "Seize them!"

The friends stood defiant. Angry stallions moved forward.

"Athos! It is acceptable," interjected Star.

Athos turned to the congregation and with a cursory nod defused the situation.

The wind stilled to a distant whisper, and the aurora disappeared. Ella surveyed the scene before her. There was Star, four stallions, the aged horse and a colt lying on the ground, smeared in what looked like blood. The first impression seemed gruesome at best.

Ella walked forward disbelievingly, to Star.

"What have you done? How could you do this to our kind? This cannot be right."

"It's not what it looks like, Ella," said Star.

"I believed you," she said sinking to the floor. All energy sapped from her body, and she began to cry, a kind of desolate sobbing that came from a horse drained of all hope. All there felt her pain.

Slowly, before her eyes, the prostrate colt got to his feet and approached her.

Ella's expression changed. Anger and sadness soon transformed to surprise and bewilderment.

Ella rose from the floor and looked at her friend.

"But I thought...the blood," she muttered.

"It's from the red berries we collected. It's part of the ancient ritual. It's there to remind us of previous atrocities committed by man and by us."

Star turned to the gathering. "Arion is pleased. The ceremony is over."

Upon Star's words, all the stallions began to disperse. He turned his attention to Ella, who was still unable to understand what had happened.

"I will explain everything," said Star softly.

The eerie moon cast a long shadow on the settling friends as the evening dissolved into the gathering velvet darkness of night time. Millions of glittering specks winked down at them like the scattered embers of a dying fire.

"It seems that Halden was a Guardian."

Bruma's eyes sprung open at the name. Halden, she thought!

"Many Guardians were sent across the lands in an attempt to find The One that would fulfil the Prophecy. Halden sent word back, many moons ago, of my existence and his conviction and belief that I was this horse. They have been waiting for me to come, ever since." continued Star.

Panic invaded her. A vision came to the old mare of that fateful night when Gaia had swapped the younglings; her dead foal. Did Star now know his origins! She began to shake uncontrollably. Her face drained. Her legs quivered, and she collapsed to the ground.

Star rushed to her side. "Mother!"

Her eyes focused. She stared anxiously into his eyes for a clue, a sign. Nothing.

Star encouraged her to her feet.

"I'm… just tired," said Bruma.

"It's been quite an ordeal for you, Mother," said Star.

"I'm fine," she replied apprehensively, still searching his face for a hint of something.

"And there's something else I found out," uttered Star, his face now grave.

Once more his gaze settled on his mother and Bruma felt sick to her stomach, her heart almost exploding from her chest as she waited for him to deliver the news that she had kept a secret all of this time.

"It's about Shade. I know where he's from," whispered Star. "This was once his herd."

The friends looked at Star in astonishment.

"Shade's herd?"

"Yes, his father was once their leader."

"W-w-what happened?" said Chub.

"Their belief in the Prophecy had thrived here since the first of their kind. They remained true to the spirit of Arion. But in time there were those who began to question its purpose. Shade's father, Balan, had knowledge of man, but unlike my time with them, it seems he was not treated kindly. Violence was his way. When he came to the Guardians, they took him in, and in time he sought to influence their thinking and through the cave pictures persuaded some, that death, sacrifice and violence was the actual way to power and that the path of healing, friendship and love was wrong and weak.

When Balan was strong enough, he took control of the Guardian herd by force. Then began a time of darkness, many hundreds of young colts were sacrificed here. The skull is a reminder to us all that death is not the way."

Star lowered his head, sadness and sorrow overcame him.

"I felt the violence of this place when we first passed here, and I feared that the rumours were true and that we were heading to something worse than even Shade."

"And now?" said Ella.

"Balan grew old, and there were those who despised what he had done in the name of Arion. Eventually, with the help of Athos, Halden and other Guardians, Balan was defeated, cast away with his only son, Shade, to roam the wilderness alone. Balan perished, and as we know, Shade made his way south. Now, order is restored."

"And the Prophecy?" said Armand.

"What about Shade, he will want his revenge?" added Tarn. "We must gather everyone together and fight him."

Star gazed ahead into the night. He didn't answer. He suddenly felt much older.

With a sigh, he turned to his friends. "I am not the son of Arion, even though they believe I am," gesturing in the direction of the Guardian herd.

"And I also know that if we are to heal these lands and help, not just our kind, but all animals, we must learn to work together. I have had this feeling all my life, that the urge to heal was the only way, and I have seen first-hand how this can bring us all, man and animal, together."

"Healing won't save us when Shade brings his army north," replied Tarn bruskly.

"Death is not the answer either!" replied Star, sharply.

"Humans sacrificed our kind, as we saw in the cave. They tried to dominate us through fear. They sought to take away our spirit and thought the gods wanted this. But each time, the will of life saved us."

"You are a coward, Star. If you do nothing, then I will." Tarn turned and bolted into the darkness.

"What will we do, Star?" said Ella disconsolately. She wanted to stay faithful to him, but part of her agreed with Tarn. The young mare probed his eyes, searching for comfort and a decisive response.

Star had nothing to offer. The frustration and weight of responsibility overwhelmed him.

"Just leave me alone," he cried suddenly, much to the shock of his friends, before galloping away.

Heads lowered, Armand, Misty, Chub and Ella wandered slowly away leaving Bruma alone staring at the monolith.

The night was clear and warm, but the old mare felt shivery. It transfixed her gaze. Tall, gnarled, almost sharp, weathered by aeons of frost, rain and summer heat, the column seemed to exude a mysterious power that she sensed.

Bruma lifted her head to the heavens. "What am I to do?" she whispered.

"What your heart says you must do," came the instant reply.

Startled, Bruma just made out the shape of another horse in the shadows of the Stone.

Athos stepped out into the moonlight where Bruma could see him clearly. His soft way soothed her troubled soul. She looked closely at him.

"You must have known the truth. Halden would have told you everything."

"You will tell him when you are ready to do so, Bruma."

"I'm afraid of what he will say. He might hate me for it. I couldn't bear that."

Athos moved closer giving her a comforting nuzzle.

"You have been the best any mother could have been for Star. He will not forsake you."

"I have wanted to tell him, many times. But somehow, I could not find the courage."

"It will come," came the reassuring reply from the old stallion.

Chapter 12

A stallion lifted his head in the morning, fearfully scenting the wind. Around him, the saffron coloured grassland quivered, and the craggy mountains blushed a deep, lush purple. He was unusually nervous having travelled alone. This time had provided him with a bewildering array of new sensations; some terrifying, others rich with wonder and delight. But although he would not have given up a single one of them to feel safer that he did, he was beginning to grow a little lonely.

A new look came to his eyes as he caught a scent on the breeze. He swung his head and instantly caught sight of another horse coming towards him. Excited at the prospect of friendship, he trotted towards her.

"Hello there," he called cheerfully.

The mare stopped, but though she too was on her own, there was little in her look that spoke of fear. She nodded her sleek head to the stallion.

"Are you alone?" asked the stallion.

"Yes," answered the mare. "You?"

The stallion nodded, and as he did so, he noticed that her right front leg was matted with blood.

"Yes, I had a fall."

"I'm sorry," said the stallion in a matter-of-fact way, common to animals, which is as much to say that a wound is a wound and there's little you can do about it so probably best not to dwell on the fact.

"It won't heal," the mare went on. "In fact, I think it's getting worse. So I'm going to see if He can help."

The stallion looked at her with a new interest.

"He?"

"The Healer, or whatever they call him."

"You mean Star," said the stallion. "I'm going to find him too."

"Are you wounded?"

"No," answered the stallion, "but I want to join up with his Band. There is danger coming."

"Yes," the mare nodded. Do you think he is the One?" she asked suddenly in a whisper. "I mean, he will save us from all this, won't he?"

"I don't know," said the stallion. "I knew him once, a long time ago. We fled the Prairie together, but I was not well, and we sought refuge at a human place. Now I choose the old way again."

"And your mother?" queried the mare.

"They took her away, one day. So I decided to leave."

"What's he like?"

"Even though he was young then, there was something about him. I heard that he denies this. He won't have any horse talk about the Prophecy. Says he is not the son of Arion. What have you heard?"

The mare shrugged.

"All I heard is that he helps animals. Not just horses but all animals. He can speak with them."

"Yes, I remember he could speak with others," said the stallion.

"Then he does have powers," replied the mare.

"But even that he denies is anything special," said the stallion, shaking his head, "or so they say. He claims that all animals can do this if they try."

"But he can heal?" asked the mare hopefully.

"Oh, yes," answered the stallion.

The mare was reassured.

"I tell you what then," said the stallion suddenly, "why don't we travel together? To be honest, I've been a little lonely since I left my Band, and four eyes are better than two. I heard wolves last night."

The mare readily agreed.

"Good, my name is Oliver," he murmured.

"And mine, Lika," she replied.

The two new companions set off across the grassland. They chatted happily in the warming sunshine as they went and soon they were delighted with the pleasure of one another's company.

*****

"So, I wanted to know if you could help," said the prairie grouse nervously. "They say you can."

She ruffled her feathers and looked up pleadingly at the stallion standing above her.

"No, I'm afraid I can't," answered the stallion falteringly, stirring in the grass. It's not me you want.

You're seeking out for Star. I saw him last over on the west hill."

The prairie grouse thanked the horse and fluttered off to find him.

Nacho shook his head, for it was a relatively new sensation to be talking with other animals like this. He wasn't very accomplished at it, but he was proud that he was one of the horses that were beginning to master it.

Nacho and the Maidens had joined with Star's herd and the Guardians after word had been sent to them and now they were settled in the valley near the Great Mountain, and as the news spread, more and more horses came to join and to flee the persecution of Shade. Their ranks had swollen to over two hundred horses.

Nacho looked across the Band and nodded as he saw the stallions away on the hill, and below them in the vast bowl of the valley, the mares grouped loosely together and set well apart. He spotted Felise among them and smiled to himself again. Since all the changes

Felise had treated him with a new respect, and he had grown very fond of her.

Nacho stirred with satisfaction as he rolled this thought in his head. He could not understand though why Star had refused the title of Leader of the Band.

Star was nearly seven years old, a sturdy, formidable looking horse and all expected him to take charge. He had if anything, since his meeting with Athos and the Guardian herd, become more of a solitary figure, spending time tending to the wounds of any animal that asked. Star showed less and less interest in spending time with his friends, much to the dismay of Ella.

Star helped and talked to the animals and tended the wounds among the stallions and mares, and they were all grateful for his strange powers. Yet, it seemed to cause Star himself nothing but pain. All of them knew better than to talk of the Prophecy that had brought him here, but for those like Athos, they were convinced of his destiny.

What does it matter if he believes or not, thought Nacho to himself? We are free of tyranny. Maybe the Prophecy has already come.

Nacho suddenly caught a scent in the air and turned to see a stallion gallop towards him.

"Well, Armand," he called with pleasure and trotted over to meet him.

"Hello, Nacho," said Armand cheerfully. "I've just been over the eastern hills, and several more horses have come in, and more join us daily. Anything from you?"

"Not really," said Nacho. "I saw Chub this morning, and he says everything is well."

"That's good," replied Armand. Nacho noticed a strain of concern play across his friend's face.

"What is it?"

"This morning, I was speaking with a couple of black headed geese by the lake, and they had heard news from the south," said Armand.

"Bad news?"

"Yes, it seems that Shade is persecuting all animals and not just us. I'm told he is coming this way too. He's on the move with a vast number under his command."

"Shade," whispered Nacho, conjuring with the name. "What's he like Armand?"

"I was young when we left," said Armand shaking his head, "but even in that time, he showed great cruelty. We have much to fear if he comes here. Do you remember those stallions that joined us recently and managed to avoid the Zellats?"

Nacho nodded gravely.

Armand continued. "They were so frightened they couldn't talk about it for moons. They say he's even developed an interest in torturing other animals. Very dark indeed."

"Has Star said anything about it?" said Nacho.

Armand paused and shook his head.

"You know how he is," answered Armand a little sadly. "I think he just wants to live a normal life and forget about Shade. I can't really blame him, given what he's been through."

"I know we have a lot to be grateful for, but Shade will come."

Armand understood the predicament they were in, but no one wanted to confront their friend with this concern.

The two stallions began to graze in the evening, and soon the simple pleasures of munching on the fresh pasture and feeling the late summer breeze on their backs had carried away all the unpleasant thoughts of Shade.

Across the valley, Misty and Ella walked together. "Will you join anyone this year," said Misty.

Ella suddenly looked a little sad. Neither Ella nor Misty had mated, which was unusual for two mares of their age not to have foaled at all yet. The various Bands across the valley were settling into a kind of normality, but their strange journey seemed to have gravely disrupted the natural rhythms of their lives.

"I don't think so," answered Ella quietly.

"But you'll have to eventually. You know Tarn is keen on you. He's very determined."

"Tarn?" snorted Ella angrily. "I'll never stand with Tarn. He's changed so much, Misty. Grown so arrogant."

"We're all changing, Ella," said Misty wistfully.

Ella smiled at her sister. "What about you?"

"I do miss him, Ella," said Misty. "Chub, I mean. I miss them all. I know when we travelled there were dangers, but we were together, now the stallions and mares have grown so far apart."

"Yes, but that's natural, now we're more settled," said Ella, "though I strangely miss the excitement of our adventures too."

Misty saw a look in Ella's eye.

"Maybe he'll come for you," she said softly.

Ella shook her head.

"No. He's so distant nowadays. Always trying to heal the animals, he doesn't seem to care or have much time for any of us anymore. He keeps telling everyone they must live in peace and friendship together. He doesn't want to fight for anything, not even me." Ella lowered her head.

"And Tarn is always jeering at him, calling him a coward. He's not a coward Misty. Why doesn't he want to be with me? I thought…" Ella broke down, and Misty comforted her.

"It's too awful the way Tarn pushes him."

"Yes," agreed Ella, "but in some strange way, I think Tarn is disappointed with him. You know how Tarn is in his ideas, and he's determined there should be a Lord of the Bands. I'm sure he wants to be Lord himself, but he's frustrated with the respect that Star still holds with everyone."

"I think he's disappointed that Star refuses to fight him for the right," said Misty.

"You know, Misty," said Ella in a whisper, "I even asked him, Star I mean. I asked him to fight for me. But he wouldn't."

Above them, the Arion star was already shining down on the valley. It shone down on Ella and Misty and Armand and Nacho on the hill, on Chub who was grazing and Tarn who was at the southern edge of the valley, gazing into the distance. It shone down on an old mare called Bruma who was lost in her own fearful thoughts and on a troubled stallion who was up on the hill talking with a prairie grouse.

"They'll be fine," said Star to the prairie grouse in a gentle voice, "as long as they get some fresh water to drink. Now I'm sorry, I have others to tend to."

"Thank you," she said as she herded her young ones away.

"You never give yourself a rest, Star."

Star swivelled around, and smiled when he saw who it was.

"Athos," he said with pleasure, "it's good to see you," Star paused.

"But I hope nothing's wrong," he added. "You're not wounded, are you?"

"No, my friend," answered the old Guardian, "though I could do with more of your company. I've hardly seen anything of you lately."

"No," said Star, "but there's so much to do, especially with so many horses joining us."

"You have a great gift, Star."

"It's nothing," answered Star immediately. "Just berries and leaves and listening to their needs."

The old horse looked intently at Star. "You cannot keep denying your destiny."

"Perhaps, but we all know instinctively what's right for us Athos."

The old Guardian nodded. He was worried about his friend, especially his denial of the Prophecy. Star himself seemed to find it so hard to live a normal life.

"You look tired," said Athos quietly.

"I've had some strange dreams lately."

"Of Arion, of the Prophecy?"

"No, about Shade. They frighten me, Athos."

Athos snorted at the very mention of his name.

"Some more horses arrived, fleeing from Shade. The news is very dark."

"I know," said Star sadly, "and not just for the horse. All animals are suffering. Some of the things I've seen…" Star sighed.

"He will come. Some say you must fight him."

"Fighting," snorted Star. "I've seen what fighting achieves. Nothing!"

The passion in his eyes surprised even Athos.

"Fight Shade, fight Tarn. Is that all we think of these days?"

"But to win your mate, is natural, is it not?" asked Athos.

"Don't you want your own Band with yearlings of your own?"

Star looked down sadly over the herds. He was thinking of Ella, and he missed her desperately.

"I don't know Athos," he said, shaking his head. "I hate everything that Shade stands for. Violence is his way."

"But surely fighting for what you love is different?"

Star looked at the old horse, his eyes lost in a bitter battle within his soul.

"I feel so confused. There is so much pain and violence in the world. I think that if Arion exists, he must be terribly cruel. Crueller than Shade, more savage even than man. We have to fight for everything, to survive. Why is this right? If I love someone and that someone loves me, then surely it is natural for us to be together. But no I have to fight for this right."

"I'm sorry Star," Athos said sympathetically. "I wish I could help you."

The two friends fell silent and made their way from the hill down into the valley. The evening was bright with a half moon rising. As they descended, they saw Chub galloping towards them.

"S-S-Star, Athos. You've got to come quickly."

"What is it, Chub?" said Athos.

"H-h-horses," said Chub in distress. He had almost lost his stutter, and it only came back when he got very excited. "They are all stallions from the south. There must be forty of them, coming up the valley."

"Zellats!" gasped Star and though he had just been talking to Athos of his hatred of fighting and violence, his first instinct drove him straight towards them.

When they reached the newcomers, they were reassured, though, for the stallions had bunched together in the middle of the herd and they seemed to be talking calmly enough to the horses who had gathered round them. Ella and Misty were there and Bruma too. Armand was running down from the hill, and Star slowed as he caught sight of Tarn standing before the newcomers.

"Are you with Shade?" he heard one of the horses shouting to the stallions.

"No," yelled a voice with pain and exhaustion.

As Star came among them, he saw in the darkness that they had been fighting. Some of them were wounded, their horse hair thick with sweat and matted blood.

"Moons ago, they came at us," the weak voice went on. "Shade and his followers. There were hundreds of them. We managed to escape, but they captured many of the mares and the younglings."

Star recognised Blake among the stallions.

"You are from Leonardo's old Band, now of Morro, are you not?"

"We are," replied Blake.

"You betrayed Leonardo and allied to Shade. Why do you now come to us?"

Blake lowered his head in shame.

"Many of us mourned the passing of Leonardo and felt the shame of what had happened. But they were too many, and Morro became our leader. In time, he too regretted his own greed. He sacrificed himself so that we might escape."

Blake's eyes fell on Star, and a great relief came over him. "So you are alive! You who came amongst us. We had hoped to find you, so the Prophecy is true."

"No, Blake. It is not the Prophecy, and I am not your Saviour."

"But we have come for your help."

"What for?"

"What do you mean what for? To fight Shade, of course."

"Fighting," said Star, shaking his head, "always fighting. How many of you are there Blake?"

"Forty-one of us survived the battle."

"So with our Bands makes perhaps two hundred stallions, many of whom are not fighters. How many Zellats would you say Shade has?"

Blake paused. He could see what Star was hinting at.

"I don't know," he muttered, hanging his head. "He has brought all the Bands together."

"I've heard his numbers are around two thousand, or maybe more?"

Blake nodded.

There was an atmosphere of fear in the air.

"But that doesn't matter," cried Blake, suddenly brightening. "The Prophecy. We'll have Arion on our side. We'll have you."

All the horses that were gathered there began to nod excitedly.

"No, Blake," cried Star, "you will not have me. I was not born to fulfil some crazy Prophecy. I will stay here with my mother and teach everyone that there is another way."

"But…" Hope drained from Blake's face.

"You are welcome to rest with us," said Star simply, "and we will tend to your wounds."

"Tend to our wounds?" snorted Blake in disgust. You mean hide here while Shade destroys everything."

"Have you forgotten your treachery in this Blake," said Star coldly, "that Morro served Shade? That when it suited your brave purpose, you handed over my friends, mothers, and my mother to Shade, without a thought for the suffering they might meet."

"It lives in our memory, to the undying shame of all of us," said Blake bitterly. "We betrayed you. But we were forced to. Morro convinced us that this was the only way to preserve the old ways. Morro was not as bad as many thought. Although he pretended to serve Shade, somewhere his heart was real. And he made a brave death."

"I'm glad to hear it," said Star with little feeling. "Did Leonardo make a brave death too?"

"Blake hung his head in shame again.

"So you won't help us," he whispered.

"I'm sorry," said Star. This time, he meant it.

"Then we are lost."

"No," cried a voice angrily, "if Star won't help you, I will."

Tarn came thundering through to the centre, his eyes blazing at Star.

"You?" said Blake, looking a little surprised.

As Tarn drew up, he turned to acknowledge Ella.

"If I can," he said.

"But will everyone follow you?" asked Blake. "You are not lord here."

"We have no lord," said Tarn with disgust. "Our venerable Star felt it unnecessary."

"No lord?" said Blake. "But, Star…"

"Star does not lead us anymore," said Tarn coldly. "He prefers looking after other animals instead of his own kind."

"Tarn," said Star quietly, "you don't know what you are saying. You cannot defeat Shade. He's too powerful. Would you lead everyone to certain death, beyond the mountain?"

"Anything is better than this slow death. We will die when he comes here anyway. I would lead those who would follow, at least then perhaps we can die with honour," cried Tarn, "like Mustangs of the Prairies. You'll come with me, won't you, Nacho? And you, Chub and Armand?"

The friends looked down in embarrassment.

"And Athos with your Guardians," said Tarn, "you'll help us, won't you?"

The old horse said nothing.

"If this is your plan," said Star calmly, "I oppose it."

"At last," snorted Tarn, swinging round suddenly towards Star. "Then fight me, Star, to see who will have the right to lead. To see if Blake shall have our help."

Star stared at Tarn but did not respond.

"So you won't fight me then?" said Tarn at last.

Star hesitated. He was fighting with himself now.

"No, I won't fight you," he answered quietly, and he turned away.

"But Star," cried Ella.

Star gave Ella a pained look. He glanced back at Chub and Armand, and at his frightened mother standing next to Athos. All the horses waited on his word.

"Blake, I will be on the hill," he muttered, "if you need me to help those wounds heal."

But Blake didn't answer. He looked coldly back at the stallion. Star paused. He felt hundreds of expectant eyes boring into him.

"What do you want from me?" he screamed with a sudden anguish.

Then Star galloped away, through the grass, up the hill.

As he went, Oliver and Lika entered the valley. They did not notice another stallion coming from the south. His face was young but with grim intent etched across it.

Chapter 13

There was nothing that either Tarn or Blake could attempt until all the stallion's wounds were healed. Besides, they had no idea what they were going to do against the might of Shade's army. However, in the suns that followed the confrontation with Star, many began to view Tarn with a new respect, and although nothing had been settled, some even began to talk of him as the lord. Many would see him standing apart with Blake, discussing matters.

Chub and Armand looked on with growing distress, for their loyalties had been torn in two. While their first allegiance was to Star, they both felt that they had some duty to help Blake as well as settle an old score for themselves for the misery Shade had inflicted on them and their families. Neither acknowledged that Tarn was some sort of lord, but they admired him for his courage, and they were both desperate to rid their world of this evil.

Of all the friends, though, Ella was the most affected. She loved Star deeply, but she could not fathom what had come of him now and why he did not want to fight for her. She knew he was in pain, but this refusal to help was worst of all. As the suns passed, Ella kept watching Tarn.

It was not that everyone was of one mind about what to do. Many of the mares that had joined and even a sizeable number of stallions agreed with Star and could see no hope of confronting Shade. Although they knew that this dark cloud was coming, for now at least there was peace, and many could see no reason to change that, just yet. It was an unsettling time for all, but many still saw a comfort and reassurance from the presence that Star brought. His healing ways with the animals seemed to bring all life closer together in harmony.

There were many to attend to after Blake's encounter with Shade's Zellats. Some wounds were deep and had grown infected. Star set to those stallions who supported him, to collecting leaves and making poultices to help their wounds heal. At first, there was resistance, but Star's touch was so gentle and their needs so great, that they grudgingly submitted to his aid and were grateful for it. Not one who had escaped from the battle in the south died of his wounds.

Star looked out on the ever-growing number of horses seeking refuge, and his heart was deeply troubled. He thought that once he had found the Guardians, everything else would fall into place. That somehow, all would make sense, and they could return to their old ways. But not so, if anything, life had become more complicated and his dream of one day returning to the safety of his beloved Prairies seemed further away now than ever.

At first, he had thought he had found the answer to his quest, here on the hill, that this had been his calling. He had denied himself the existence of the Prophecy and eventually had found a way to be free once more. But as he tried to build this life again, he realised that the violence that so terrified him, of Zell and Shade and that which he had smelt on the jaws of the wolves when they had chased him, dwelt deep in his heart too.

He had sensed it first when he was a youngling, that time when he had helped Chub at the river, that welling anger when Kraal had tried to bully his friend, and he had defended him. For deep down, Star too wanted to test himself against other stallions, as was nature's way, to fight for his own Band and to make his stand, to fight for Ella. Yet, as a healer now, he felt his place was to help animals, not to harm them.

Many times Star thought of the Prophecy and shook his head. So much of it seemed genuine, so much impossible. But deep inside, Star was somewhat glad that his confusion meant that he could ignore those words that Halden had first mouthed in his stories. For with the years, he had begun to think more and more of the line of the Prophecy that made him tremble, "Sacrifice shall be his meaning."

He was thinking of those words now as Athos came ambling towards him. His expression was grave.

"I've found you at last," said the old horse quietly as he arrived.

"I've been collecting berries and herbs," began Star, as cheerfully as he could.

"Star," interrupted Athos, "the others asked me to find you and tell you. They're moving south. Tarn is leading them."

"They'll be destroyed," said Star quietly, "is that what they want?"

"I'm sorry for you, Star," said the old sage softly as he gazed into Star's eyes. "There is something else also. Ella has agreed to join with Tarn."

Star looked back at his friend but said nothing.

"Misty too."

"But they can't," cried Star with horror, "not Ella and Misty."

That's what they plan to do."

"Thank you for telling me," said Star sadly.

"Star," cried Athos suddenly, "you must choose. Decide to help them or not. Or fight Tarn for Ella. But you cannot continue to live like this."

Star fell silent.

"The Prophecy is real, and you cannot avoid your destiny forever."

Athos turned, and Star watched his friend walk away. He felt desperately alone. He looked across the hills, and Tarn was moving slowly down the slope. In the valley below, horses waited for him, and by his side, Star recognised the companion of his youth, Ella.

"We're all here," Tarn said as he reached the assembled horses. It was a ragged looking bunch. "How many have we persuaded to come?"

"All of my stallions," answered Blake, "and with your thirty horses, that makes about eighty."

"If Star had been with us we could have trebled that," said Tarn bitterly.

"We've managed to persuade another twenty or so, but the rest are afraid of Shade and listen to Star."

"It's a pity Nacho won't come," said Blake. "But he won't leave Star."

Ella looked sadly at Tarn as they talked of Star. But she knew that her duty lay with her friends.

"I wish he would change his mind," said Blake. "Even if this Prophecy isn't real, to have him with us would lift everyone's moral. If the Zellats heard of it, maybe some of them might desert Shade."

"Our best plan is to try to get as close to Shade as possible," said Tarn, "like we discussed. Then if a group of us can infiltrate the herd and kill him…"

Blake nodded though the thought of what lay ahead of them filled none of the horses with any confidence. Tarn saw the look in their eyes and tried to lift their spirits.

"Armand and Chub, take a few stallions and scout ahead as we travel. It is essential that we are not seen."

Chub and Armand nodded their heads.

"But have we time to say goodbye to him?" said Ella.

Tarn looked keenly at Ella.

"Yes," he said at last, "but you must hurry, we're leaving before daybreak. Winter is coming."

The friends looked at each other almost guiltily. None of them really believed that this was where their journey with Star was to end.

"Ella," said Tarn, "you don't have to come, you know. It will be no place for a mare. Stay safe here."

Suddenly, Ella's eyes blazed.

"Tarn," she said frostily, "do you think I fear danger, after all we've been through?"

"And you Misty," said Tarn.

"I'll go where my sister goes," said the mare, though she was looking at Chub.

*****

When Ella found him, Star was on his own ruminating sadly. Misty, Chub and Armand had already said their farewells and Star looked deeply distressed. Again he tried to dissuade his friends from going, but it had been to no avail.

"Star," called the mare quietly as she walked up to him.

Star turned his head immediately. "Ella."

"Star, I have come to say…"

"I know," said Star as he moved closer. "I wish I could say something…"

"You can't Star, I've decided. My duty lies with my friends and as you would not fight for me… with Tarn also."

Star smiled almost bitterly

"He's a good stallion."

"He's brave," said Ella coldly, looking intently at Star, "and he has a good heart."

Star nodded.

"But you have a good heart too, Star," said Ella suddenly, "and you were brave. Once. I would have stood with you. If…if only you…"

Star winced, but he didn't answer her.

"Why don't you come with us, Star? We'll fight Shade together."

"You can't fight Shade like that," answered Star. "That's what he wants. Besides, I'm tired of fighting."

"But they need your help," said Ella.

"All animals need my help."

"Since when did others become more important than your own kind? And what of the Prophecy?"

"The Prophecy is a lie. What has it given us but misery."

"But can't you see Star, many of the Guardians believe you are the One, that it is true. They need to believe it. At least it gives them hope. With you leading us, perhaps we could have a chance."

"A chance to do what? To destroy our herd."

"There is no herd, no Band. The best of us refused to lead," said Ella scornfully.

Ella faltered as Star looked intently into the mare's bold and beautiful eyes, and in their glitter, he caught a hardness that came close to contempt. But again he said nothing.

"I was right," said Ella at last, shaking her head.

"Right?"

"To accept Tarn. At least he acts like a stallion."

Now it was Star's turn to grow angry.

"Then he can die with all the other stallions too."

Ella stared back at Star, her eyes flaming.

"You're a coward, Star," she cried furiously, turning on her haunches, "a coward."

"Ella," whispered Star.

But she was gone.

As Ella, Tarn and the others left a sudden cry shook the air, and they paused and looked back at the hill. Star was above them. He rose on his hind legs, threw his head back and let out another cry, bitter and lonely and so full of pain that every horse stopped to listen. Then suddenly, Star turned and ran, as fast as he could, away from that place and into the rain that had begun to sheet through the evening.

Star ran through the night and didn't stop until morning came, bleak and grey and with little welcome. His thoughts had exhausted him as he tried to shut out the guilt that was threatening to overwhelm him. Eventually, sleep came to him and a strange dream. Star murmured painfully in his sleep.

He was standing next to a modest log building, deserted, open landscape all around. A simple slanted wooden cross denoted a single grave that stood out against the barren wilderness, weathered and worn by nature's harshness. He had never been here before, but somehow he recognised the place, and as he looked more intently towards the cross it began to glow, and a voice whispered across the wind.

"Star," it said, "Star, you have nearly learnt all. But before you can fulfil the Prophecy, you must know the secret. Then you will know what to do."

Star woke with a shudder. The morning had hardly advanced, but the troubled horse got to his feet and ran on. It was approaching evening, three suns later, when Star finally got back to his Band. He paced restlessly towards the mares. He was looking for Bruma.

He found his mother overlooking the valley from a steep vantage point, on her own. She looked older than he remembered and Star suddenly felt desperately sorry for the mare. The stallion had neglected her in the past few seasons while he had spent much of his time with other animals and the sick and he realised that he had not visited her in a while.

"Mother," he said quietly as he padded up.

"Star," said Bruma, "Star is that you?"

"Yes, Mother, how are you?"

"Well enough," whispered the concerned mare, "and you, Star?"

"Well enough too," said Star sadly, "though Tarn has won Ella. They have gone south to fight Shade. I fear for them, Mother."

Bruma stirred. She recognised the names, but in her confused thoughts, she could hardly recall who Tarn and Ella were.

"Mother," Star went on suddenly, "will you tell me about my father, about, Abrazo? You've never really talked about him."

The mare blinked back nervously at Star.

"I want to know about him," said Star, "all about him. His bravery, I wish I'd met him, Mother. I wish he were here now. There are so many things I'd ask him. What he thought of the Prophecy of Arion."

Star had wandered away a little from Bruma. "Mother, why don't you come down to the valley. It's dangerous and slippery here."

"I can see things more clearly from here, Star," she replied.

Star had his back to the mare. His voice broke into his thoughts, but suddenly Bruma wasn't listening anymore. Her dim senses had been roused by something stirring nearby, behind some tall boulders. In the corner of her eye, she saw a young stallion, and he was watching Star intently.

"I wish I could understand what is required of me. I'm sure he could have advised me," Star went on as Bruma's attention focused more intently on the skulking stallion. She sensed danger as she moved slowly towards Star again.

"I'm sure he would have told me what to do about Shade. Whether I should fight or not."

But Bruma couldn't hear him anymore. The stallion by the rocks moved slowly from his place of cover and without a sound he charged towards Star who was near the cliff edge. The old mare wanted to stamp, to cry out, but she found herself choked, paralysed with fear.

Suddenly, Star heard a cry, and a flurry of dust flew up around him. Bruma leapt forward and clattered into the on-coming stallion. Both lost their footing and plunged over the edge.

Momentarily blinded, he steadied himself. His mother had vanished. Then to his horror, his gaze took him into the valley below. Two horses lay prone.

Star's eyes flashed with despair. "Mother!" he cried galloping down the ravine face to her stricken body.

"Mother!" cried Star, running to her aid as she lay on the valley floor.

Nearby, the broken, dead body of the assassin was splayed across a jagged boulder, eyes open but unseeing, his mouth slightly open, a fat purple tongue hanging out. He lay at an unnatural angle, legs splayed out, and his back painfully arched, as though someone had just tossed the horse aside like an unwanted rag doll. Star turned back to his mother. "What happened?" The stallion's face was racked with grief trying to make sense of everything.

"I don't know," whispered Bruma, her breath pained and rasping. "He came from behind the rocks. He must have been sent to harm you."

"To harm me?" said Star. "But who?"

"Shade," whispered Bruma. "Shade sent him."

"Why now?"

"Star, listen to me," said Bruma suddenly, flexing in pain. "There is little time, and there is something I must tell you."

Bruma's eyes were suddenly bright as though the shock of her fall had swept years of darkness from her clouded mind.

"What do you mean little time?" said Star.

"I am dying, Star, my body is broken."

"No, Mother," cried Star, "I will heal you."

"No, Star, not even you can do that this time."

"But Mother…"

"I am not your mother, Star."

Star stopped. He stared at Bruma in blank amazement.

"I don't understand… Not my mother?"

"No," whispered Bruma and as he listened, it seemed she was telling him something he had known all along. "You were changed at birth."

"Then who," gasped Star.

"Gaia, Gaia is your real mother, Star. The mare you said goodbye to all those years ago. Zell and Shade killed your father, Abrazo."

"Shade killed my father."

"Yes, Star. He destroyed everything."

"Shade," whispered Star, his voice trembling.

"That night, Shade and the Zellats were coming to kill you, so Halden and Gaia switched you with my dead foal."

"A changeling child will be awoken," gasped Star. "Then the Prophecy…"

"Oh, Star," gasped Bruma bitterly, "I'm so sorry I didn't tell you sooner. But I wanted to protect you."

Bruma stopped talking. She could hardly speak anymore. Blood sputtered from her mouth. The stallion gazed at her. There was a long silence. Then his anger burst to the surface.

"But… Bruma, you should have told me," he said bitterly.

"I know, Star," gasped the dying mare, "but I didn't want anything to harm you. For I have loved you like a mother…"

Bruma winced in agony.

Star stepped forward, and very gently he dipped his head towards the mare and licked her muzzle.

"I know," he said tenderly, "and you were the most wonderful mother…"

"Oh, my, Star."

Bruma's body began to shake. Star looked to the sky, his bitter eyes flaming with contempt. "I thought you were a God of healing, but you are no better than man. Is suffering all you see. Death is all around us, and you do nothing to help."

Bruma caught the rage in his face. "What are you going to do?" questioned the concerned mare weakly.

"I'm going to fight. I'm going to find Tarn, Ella and the others. I'm going to do my best to save them, and I'm going to kill Shade and avenge my father."

"But, Star. There are too many of them."

"Then I will die well. Isn't that what he wants." He turned his rage to the heavens once more. "Well? Isn't this what you want? Sacrifice shall be my meaning!"

Bruma was staring helplessly at Star. She was growing delirious, and she no longer knew what Star was saying.

"Goodbye Star," she whispered, "I hope in time you will understand. Forgive me."

"Bruma," cried Star, "wait, I will heal you."

But it was over. Bruma was dead.

The grief came to Star in waves and threatened to consume him entirely. It was his master, for now. He was at its mercy, and at times it gnawed at him with such ferocity he feared for his sanity.

An all-consuming feeling of hatred built in his heart, and as he thought of Shade and his father and Ella, violence swelled inside. But with that terrible anger that now burned in him came something he had never experienced before, clarity. He suddenly realised that this feeling was different. It was not a sense of vengeance but a desire for justice.

A wise old horse had been observing all this time, watching the situation unfold and he saw the change of recognition in the stallion's face, and he knew that Star, was ready to accept the Prophecy and his destiny was set.

"Star," said Athos quietly.

Star gathered himself, caught off guard by the old sage. He turned to face the Guardian, a new proud strength and confidence in him.

"There is a dark secret that Shade hides. A secret that he would wish no one else to find, for in doing so and exposing his heinous crime, his true madness would be revealed."

"What is this secret, Athos?"

"Shade and his father, Balan were defeated as you know and so ended a dark time in our history. His lust for blood was driven by the conviction that his actions of sacrifice would empower him, just like the humans in the cave pictures. That in some way violence would give him power over all animal kind because humankind was powerful.

Banished forever, Balan and Shade wondered the wilderness. Balan died, and Shade found sanctuary with humans. But his father's madness was deep rooted in his son and Shade now harboured thoughts even to control man."

"But how?" Star questioned.

"He sought to sacrifice human. He killed a child and worse, tried to eat her heart and by doing so thought he would take on the invincibility of their kind."

Star's face was etched with horror. There was an unwritten lore amongst animals forbidding this, for all understood the madness such an act would bring.

Star then gasped in recognition. "My dream. I saw this in my dream. A wooden house a human burial place…"

A renewed hope flowed through Star's veins, a weakness had been found. His heart soared once more.

"To the Great Spirit, first in all things, creator of all life, who was and is and always will be. You are present with us here and now, at this moment. Forgive me for doubting you. I offer myself to do your bidding. Give me an open heart, made strong with love, a mind clear and wise with understanding. Help give me the courage to fulfil my destiny."

Star turned intently to Athos. "Send word to the four corners, to all kind."

Athos looked contented. "Then, you believe."

Star nodded. "Though I still fear where it will lead. Now we must also hurry and stop the others reaching Shade first. Gather the rest of our forces."

Star's mind was filled with thoughts of Ella and his friends, and though he still had no real plan, he was desperate that he should be in time to help them. But something else clouded his mind, something in the Prophecy.

No matter thought Star now. If I must be the sacrifice then, I shall willingly.

Star looked up at the heavens.

"Arion, you must guide me now, for I give myself to you and carry out your will, whatever that might be."

The wind moaned around Star's head, and suddenly he felt less alone.

Chapter 14

The weather was unusually warm, and in the rare stillness, a strange haze hung over the land, as Tarn and his followers came down off the slopes of the mountain range. The sky was cloudless, and though the coming of the drying grass moon had weakened the strength of the sun's rays, it still exuded warmth more reminiscent of a summer's day than that of autumn. It gave the horses little pleasure, however, for there was a fear in their tread as they looked out into the day. Tarn and Blake walked at the front of the column, occasionally pausing to survey the land before them. If they expected to have a fight at any moment, now at least their fear was premature, for there were no Zellats in sight.

Suddenly, a small group of stallions came running towards them.

"Chub," cried Tarn as they ran up, "what signs?"

"It's odd," answered Chub, nodding his head in salute, "But there's no sign at all of the Zellats. We picked up some a while back, but they were very old."

"But I thought Shade was moving north?" said Blake, shaking his head.

"Have you noticed the stillness?" said Armand suddenly. He had been walking behind Blake.

"Yes," answered Tarn, "I think we all have."

"It's eerie," said Armand, "like a kind of emptiness."

"I think I know what it is," said Ella. "Have you noticed how few animals there are around?"

Tarn nodded his head gravely.

"Yes, yes I have. It's as though they've all run away. Well, we must be on our guard, and we should try to find some tree cover as soon as possible."

Chub, Armand and the others set off once more. It was late in the day when they came upon a small copse of trees. The sun was trying to draw back the last of its amber strands over the horizon as the pomegranate sky cast an unnerving colour over the landscape.

Armand and Chub walked together. Both shared the confused feeling of fear and excitement as the eighty horses began to tread through the trees.

"Armand," whispered Chub, "I know we are told as stallions to face fear and not shrink from it, but is it all right to feel like I'm feeling? I mean, to be a little… nervous."

Armand smiled.

"Of course it is Chub," he said. "I feel the same."

"Really?"

"Yes. And it's natural. I'm sure even the Gods have been frightened at some point. I think it shows us the importance of valuing fear," said Armand, "for keeping us wary. It keeps us alive."

"What do you think Tarn has got in mind?" asked Chub quietly.

"You heard what he said, about getting close to Shade. Beyond that, I don't know."

"If ever there was a time that we needed Arion." replied Chub.

"I-I-I wish Star were with us, I feel better somehow when he's around." continued Chub.

"I know, Chub," Armand nodded sadly. "But we're on a different journey now. Star made his choice, and I can't blame him."

"But if the Prophecy were true…"

"But it's not. It's just a story, like all the stories we heard. So we shall have to be brave my friend and fight Shade without his help."

Chub's spine tingled, but suddenly there was a loud squeal from up ahead. One of the stallions reared in the air, clearly terrified by the sight before him as if boxing with some imaginary opponent. Armand and Chub galloped forward and gasped at the sight of what had startled him.

There in the darkening clearing, strewn across the ground and hanging from brittle branches, were animals of various sizes. They were all dead, mutilated. There were prairie dogs, grouse, voles, ferrets and a fox cub, lying on the earth and hanging skewered on a nearby branch was a young beaver. The stench of death hung everywhere.

Chub and his friends trembled as they looked on at that grisly scene.

"What's happened here?" cried Tarn furiously.

"Shade," whispered Blake.

Amid the choking smell of decay, the horses caught a faint scent of their own kind hanging in the still air, and they knew that the Zellats had been here.

It's terrible," whinnied Ella. "What is he doing to our world?"

"That must be why there are so few animals about," Chub quivered. "They are f-f-fleeing from Shade."

"It seems that Shade is not just content with ruling our kind. He wants to control all animal kind," pondered Armand.

"Shade," said Tarn bitterly. "I didn't think even he could sink to this. Well, let him come, for when I meet him, he shall pay dearly for this."

The disturbing incident, far from frightening them, seemed to stir a fury and determination in their hearts.

They rested that night on the edge of a forest and the next morning plunged into a deeply wooded valley that was cut by a series of streams. Strangely for the season, they were not as fast flowing, and it was clear that there had been little rain in many suns. A sense of foreboding was growing in their hearts as they travelled with no sign of other animals about them. Armand was banking the far hill when he called to the others.

"Quiet," he rasped, as loudly as he dared.

Ella and Tarn were the first to reach Armand, who was gazing down into the next valley. Wider than the one they had just crossed, it was even more heavily wooded on its far slopes and through the middle of it, ran an earth track.

"Shade?" whispered Tarn, as the rest of the party crested the hill.

Armand shook his head.

"No," listen.

The horses listened intently, and soon they caught on the wind the sound that Armand had heard.

The horses began to back away in the grass.

"Hide," ordered Tarn.

They did as they were told and it wasn't long before they saw them.

A caravan of many hundreds; men, mostly elderly, women and crying children and babies, desperate and exhausted, heads bowed, a broken people. Sickness was in the air. Dogs barked and growled under the heavy packs they carried. Every available horse was loaded with the old or wounded in makeshift travois' whose wooden poles hissed and scraped along the rough terrain.

Tarn's Band stirred fretfully in the grass as the column came on. But if they were frightened of being seen they needn't have worried, for the Lakota were more concerned about the pursuing bluecoats. Their heads and hearts were too full of fear to give any time for Tarn and his friends.

"Where are they going?" whispered Misty.

"I don't know, but I have seen their kind before. These people saved Star and Star told me many stories of war with the white skinned humans," said Ella.

"This land is sick. Pain and sadness live not just in our world," pondered Armand.

North went the column, and the horses watched until the last of them disappeared over the ridge, and their strange sounds were lost on the wind.

The horses did not notice that from the far side of the hill, as they watched the Lakota, a group of stallions watched them too.

They crossed the valley themselves and entered the far trees. Now Chub and Blake went ahead to scout, while the others wove on slowly through the trees. It was nearly dark when Ella strayed into a thick clump of undergrowth and started, for something was moving beneath her. Suddenly, a little grey, brown flecked head with long ears and large shining eyes popped up from the drying leaves, and when it saw Ella, its eyes flashed with fear. It sprang away and darted and skittered back and forth desperate to escape, but at each turn, it was confronted by another horse. Again it turned and swivelled, once again its exit was blocked.

The animal seemed in a frenzy of terror.

"You there," called Armand, "don't be frightened."

The creature cowered, quivering, his nose twitching uncontrollably.

"Don't be frightened, I said. We don't want to hurt you."

Once more the creature tried to break for freedom, once more it failed, then turning to the horses, a little fear went out of his eyes as the steady realisation came to him that he was indeed in no harm.

"What do you want?" said the prairie hare.

"Nothing," said Armand.

"Your kind always want something, usually to hurt us animals."

"We don't want to hurt you," insisted Armand quickly. "It's other horses that do that, not us."

"So, you are not with him?" whispered the creature. "Shade."

"No, we are not with Shade."

The hare seemed to relax considerably. Ella and Misty had come up now, and the rest of the group pressed into the circle to try to get a look, fascinated by the sight of Armand, talking to another animal.

"Who are you?" asked Armand.

"I am Hulver. I'm a hare," answered the creature as he was grooming his long ears. "I'm hiding."

"From Shade?"

Hulver nodded sadly.

"But who are you if you are not with Shade," he said suddenly, "and what are you doing here?"

"We've come to find Shade," answered Armand.

"Find Shade?" whispered the hare, sucking in his breath. "But why would you want to find him. All the animals flee Shade."

"To kill him," answered Armand simply.

The hare's nose twitched quizzically as he stared at the horse, then his big bright eyes glinted excitedly.

"Kill him? Then it's true, what all the animals are whispering."

"What's true?"

"The Prophecy."

Armand looked at Ella with amazement.

"They say he comes to save us all. For many suns, rumours have been spreading across the lands. He's our only hope."

Again Armand looked at Ella, and both of them felt a quickening in their hearts.

"Do you know where Shade is?" asked Armand.

"Oh, yes. He is very close. If you…"

As the hare began to explain, some of the stallions stirred expectantly. They could not understand what the creature was saying, but they could see from Armand's expression that something vital was being discussed.

"What is it Armand?" one asked eagerly when the hare had finished.

Armand shook his head gravely, and the others pressed in to listen.

"Shade. He's just two suns away, to the south, with many, many horses. They have settled around a small lake. There are some three thousand of them. From the sounds of it, Shade has his Zellats in training all the time. He sends them out in large groups to terrorise other animals and practice their viciousness…"

Armand's voice dropped to a whisper. He looked sadly at his friends.

"They are killing everything. Just like we saw in the clearing. The animals believe that Shade wants to exterminate them all. The madness has him."

The horses shuddered.

"Then we must strike quickly," said Tarn suddenly, "for all our sakes."

"It's going to be hard," said Armand. "We'll have to get through the Zellats for a start. And then it seems he's guarded day and night."

"But we will have the element of surprise," said Tarn. "Shade is not expecting anything, least of all an attack right at the heart of his power base. Besides, I'm convinced that not all these horses outside of the Zellats truly follow Shade, if we can turn enough of them, we might stand a chance."

Tarn looked gravely at his friends, each of them understanding the suicidal consequences.

"We must do this and darkness will be our best hope. Travel in stealth. Use our instincts to find a way through."

The others nodded, but with that, they heard a noise up ahead. Something was approaching fast through the trees. The horses readied themselves, but before Tarn could issue an order, Blake came crashing through the branches.

"Chub," he whinnied as soon as he saw Tarn, "they've got Chub."

"Who? Who has?" said Tarn.

"Zellats," panted Blake. "They took us by surprise. We'd come to the top of a small hill, and Chub told me to wait while he ran ahead, but as soon as he got to the bottom of the valley, they came from nowhere. There must have been twenty of them. There was nothing I could do."

"Then we must rescue him," said Armand.

"They're moving fast," said Blake. "They'll probably be back with Shade before we can catch them."

"But we've got to try."

"Did they see you, Blake? asked Tarn suddenly.

"No" answered Blake, "we were shielded by a copse."

"Then maybe they still don't know we're here," said Tarn unconvincingly.

"Well, they'll know soon enough," cried Armand, already preparing to set off.

"Wait, Armand," said Tarn, "you mustn't be so hasty. Our greatest hope now is the element of surprise, and they still don't know we're here. But if we go blundering into camp to rescue Chub, it could ruin everything. Think, Armand."

Armand paused.

"But we've got to do something. I'll steal in at night."

"Yes, it's possible," said Tarn, "but we must be careful. I wish there were an easy way for us to get into his camp."

"There is."

Tarn swung round to find Ella standing behind him with Misty next to her. He blinked with surprise.

"We could go," said Ella calmly, "Misty and me." Their mares will likely not care for the Zellats. We could mingle with them, who would notice?"

"No, Ella," said Tarn immediately, "I won't hear of it."

"Why not?" said Ella. "What notice will the Zellats take of two mares moving through three thousand horses? At least we can find out where they're holding Chub, at best try to rescue him. Besides, somebody needs to find out about Shade."

Again, Tarn shook his head.

"No, Ella, I'm not putting you in danger."

"Then why did you let us come?" snorted Ella. "To tend to the wounded perhaps, or watch you all die?" No, Tarn, we came to help you fight Shade, and though you may think we are not as strong, our courage is just as great."

Tarn looked at Ella's beautiful face and bold eyes and was silent.

"Besides, said Ella, "There's something else I want to do. If I can get into their camp, I want to try to find my mother."

Both Tarn and Armand felt a tightening in their gut, for they hardly dared think of their mothers and whether or not Shade had put them to death after their escape.

"But Ella…" said Tarn.

"It's settled then," she said. "Blake, can you show us where they captured Chub? We'll pick up their tracks and follow them straight to the camp."

Tarn could see the determination on Ella's face and realised it was pointless arguing with her.

"Very well, Ella," he relented at last, "then listen to me. If you can get into their camp, you must do as I say. Find out where they're keeping Chub and anything you can about Shade, then get away again. We'll need to arrange a meeting point. Armand, ask Hulver how well he knows the countryside around here."

Armand nodded and turned to the hare.

"But, Ella," Tarn went on, "you must promise me not to try anything foolish."

Ella looked back at Tarn, smiled and nodded.

"Hulver says there's a good spot where we can wait," said Armand. "He says there's a small horseshoe canyon, a quarter of a sun from Shade's herd. There's plenty of water. It's a good hiding place for all of us, but we'll need to be vigilant, it's a dead end, and the slopes are very steep, so the moment we sense danger we have to leave there."

"Very well," said Ella, "we'll meet you there. Hulver can tell us how to find it. Now we must hurry. Blake, show us where you lost Chub."

Ella spent a few moments talking to the hare and then, nodding gravely, she took her farewell of Tarn and Armand. She and Misty turned with Blake and ran off into the evening.

The rest of the Band watched them go, tilting their heads with a mixed sense of pride and sadness.

Chapter 15

Shade lowered his head and took in a great gulp of water through his thin lips, then, looking around the lake at the massed horses about him as far as the eye could see, he sighed with a grim satisfaction.

Star, he thought, was probably dead now at the hands of his assassin and the Zellats were prepared and baying for blood. Animals were suffering at the hands of his brutal followers. His ambitious plan to control all appeared to be unstoppable. Shade smiled as he thought of the orders he had given to exterminate every living thing. It took him back to all those years ago, to the day when the wolf had taken his eye after the humans came hunting for him on his escape south. But, escape he did and found his place with the Prairie herds under the protection of Zell. But the madness grew and eventually consumed him. Now he would take his revenge on everyone.

"Soon," he mumbled quietly to himself, a flaming insanity in his eye, "soon, even mankind will tremble before me, and my vengeance will be complete. They'll all pay for what they did. Father, I will honour your name."

His thoughts turned north, and again his mind thought of Star.

"The Healer. Isn't that what they call him?" snorted Shade with disgust. "So has my assassin done his work or is Star skulking in fear?"

Shade suddenly felt strangely unnerved. He often thought of Star now and even dreamt of him. Although he told himself there was no truth in the Prophecy, those thoughts always made him nervous. Somewhere deep inside him, there was a niggling doubt, some secret voice that kept whispering to him. Shade kept the voices at bay, but still the doubts came.

He looked up. Caius was coming towards him. When Caius got to the Zellat bodyguard, he stopped, and exchanged a few words with them, then came straight to his master.

"Lord," he said. "More word of the humans. The men in blue coats are everywhere. They seek the black haired people."

"When I was younger, Caius," Shade muttered, "the white skinned man killed many of the black haired people. Bloodshed, that's what man is best at. That's what I learnt from him."

Caius looked keenly at his master. He had never heard Shade talk of man in this way.

"You, Lord?" he whispered. "You have a knowledge of man?"

Typically, such impertinent questioning would have brought an angry response, but Shade was feeling indulgent.

"Yes, Caius. An excellent knowledge."

Caius waited as his master took another drink from the lake water.

"But I never knew," said Caius quietly when Shade raised his head again.

"You never needed to know. These things are best kept secret from the herds."

Caius stirred. He felt deeply privileged to be allowed into his master's confidence.

"But don't you fear them, Lord? Humans, I mean."

"Fear is for weaklings, Caius. Haven't I taught you that yet? No, I don't fear man. I admire him, especially the white skin. They take what they want and kill everyone that gets in their way. The white man is a thinker also and has power over animals. They are the bringer of violence and violence gives victory, if you know how to use it."

Now Caius shifted uncomfortably. Though Caius was no stranger to violence, to talk of man in this way sounded like a kind of sacrilege.

"How does man tell us about violence?"

"Man shows us how to master and direct it. There is violence in all things, Caius, but most creatures are slaves to it. But man is no one's slave and so can use violence as he wills. To take what we want, we must be ruthless like him."

Caius looked at his master in amazement, and he suddenly felt a shiver run down his spine.

With that, there was a pained squeal, and both Shade and Caius looked across the herd. Near the western end of the lake, they could see a group of

Zellats shouting and taking turns kicking and jostling an older stallion.

"Go on, kick him again," cried one of the Zellats, as another launched himself forwards. When he neared the stallion, he turned and kicked out with his back legs. The victim swung round and reared at the horse in fury and frustration.

"That's how we Zellats treat traitors," they sneered.

"Go on, kick him again," they cried out, "bite him hard, and make Morro suffer."

Another Zellat ran forward to kick the stallion, and again Morro swung round and missed. He lifted his pained face, exhausted, but there was little he could do against his captors. Morro couldn't see them; he was blind.

Among the main herd, straddled across the grasslands, hundreds of mares grazed, disgruntled, under the unnaturally warm day.

There were times of the day when they would drift together and looking about nervously, snatch a few moments of greedy conversation. Pretending all the while to feed, they would whisper to each other.

"When are we going north?" whispered one.

"Who knows," said another. "When Shade decrees it."

"Then maybe that Zellat filth might stop throwing their weight around us all." said a third.

"Shhh," whispered the first mare, you'd better be careful what you say. They don't mind killing anyone male or female who speaks out against Shade."

"I don't care. I hate them, and Shade."

The others blinked fearfully.

"I don't know why we accept it," the mare went on.

"But what can we do?" said the first horse. "Shade's power is absolute."

"But there are many of the mares and even some of the stallions that have grown to hate him," said another. "I've heard them talking when they dare."

"And it's more than their life's worth. Shade had ten of them killed last week. His Zellats are fiercely loyal to him. They never stop hunting down traitors. No, nothing can challenge Shade now."

"I put my faith in Him," said the last mare quietly.

"Who?"

"The one in the north."

The mares fell silent, a furtive glance from side to side just to make sure none had been heard.

"He will sacrifice himself to free us all," whispered the mare. That is what He, was born for."

"Don't talk like that, you'll get us all killed," whinnied one of the group.

"Well," I believe that he will come to fulfil the Prophecy and free us all. I heard he was born on the Prairies amongst some of us and fled a long time ago."

"What's that?" came a voice from behind them. The mares stared but when they turned it wasn't Zellats they saw but another female.

They all recognised her for she was famous in the herd, but they were surprised to see her amongst them now. Shade kept her at his side perpetually, but in the past suns, Shade had been busy with thoughts of the march, and Gaia had persuaded him to allow her to wander for a little while every sundown with the herd. She had just been to see Rosa and Aiko and was walking back when she overheard part of their conversation.

"Nothing," said the mare that had been speaking, dropping her eyes guiltily.

"Come, my dear," said Gaia, "I know you were saying something."

They looked uncertainly at one another.

"Please don't tell Shade," said the first mare. "If you do we wouldn't…"

"Don't worry," said Gaia gently, "I will tell Shade nothing, nothing at all. I promise."

The mare who had first spoken of the Prophecy looked intently at Gaia before continuing.

"He's coming," she said, "to free us all and fulfil Prophecy."

"Ah," said Gaia sadly, "I thought that's what you were saying."

"Have you heard it too?" said the mare. "Do you know the Prophecy?"

"Oh, yes, I know it." Gaia smiled.

"But do you think it's true?"

"Go on believing it, my dear, if it gives you hope," said Gaia quietly as she turned and walked slowly away.

As she went, Gaia shook her head. 'Poor things,' she thought to herself sadly. 'If they only knew that my Star is dead. But they need something to believe in. It can do them no harm.'

As Gaia thought now of Star, she felt that familiar anguish in her heart. With the years, the pain of loss and grieving had hardly grown fainter. She could still picture Star in her mind's eye. His little face blinking up at her in the night. It was too cruel. Her beautiful son trampled to death by buffalo.

Star was gone, and Abrazo was gone. Halden too. Only Aiko and Rosa remained as a fragile link to her past. She had told them both the truth about Star and the night of his birth. Many times in the past suns she had asked them to recount the story of their journey and dwelt lovingly on their descriptions of Star as he began to grow. But the stories always ended in the same way. In the pained silence of the mares as she asked them about the day he died.

Gaia looked across the lake and spotted Shade with Caius. The hatred she felt for him swelled in her stomach as she watched a party of Zellats gallop towards him. They were escorting another horse who looked vaguely familiar to her.

"Lord Shade," cried one of the Zellats, rushing ahead.

"What is it now?" snapped Shade irritably, furious at being interrupted.

"To the north," panted the stallion, "a sun away. Stallions."

Caius looked at his master.

"Well?" said Shade.

"They came from the direction of the mountains," said the stallion nervously. "They are not ours."

"Are you certain?"

"Yes, my Lord. We have followed them since they crossed the Range."

"Was, He among them?" pressed Shade.

"No. I'm sure of it," said the Zellat confidently.

"Definitely?"

"Yes," he responded.

Shade nodded to himself. He was pleased.

"How many?" he asked.

Maybe eighty or so. No more than that anyway."

"Eighty come to face our thousands. They're certainly brave, I'll give them that."

"Lord Shade," said the Zellat, looking back towards his companions, "we captured one of them."

"Bring him," said Caius immediately.

The Zellats called to the others, and the stallion they had been escorting was pushed forward. His face was badly bruised, and there were cuts around his eyes.

"You," said the leader, as soon as he saw Chub.

Chub glared furiously at Shade as the leader eyed him.

"You've grown, I see."

Chub said nothing.

"So tell me, why are you here? Why have you all come?"

Again Chub was silent.

"Come now, you must want something. Did Star send you?"

Chub's eyes flickered, for he was amazed that Shade knew that Star was still alive. But as soon as he had been captured by the Zellats, Chub had determined that silence was his only course of action.

"Still dumb," snorted Shade. "No matter. Your master is probably dead by now, and the Zellats will soon loosen your tongue. Take him away and guard him carefully until I have time to come."

The Zellats moved in around Chub.

"And don't think of trying to escape," said Shade. "You may have succeeded once but to do so again would cost dearly, as did those two mares that day."

Chub swung his head up.

"What do you mean?" he whispered.

"They paid with their lives," said Shade. "What were their names, Caius?"

"Luna… Luna and Fauna."

"Ah, yes."

"You killed them?" gasped Chub, his legs beginning to shake.

"No," said Shade, smiling, "you killed them. And if you try anything there are always the other two. Aiko and Rosa."

Chub felt the shock of his mother's name like a physical blow.

"Take him away," cried Shade.

"What shall we do about the others, Lord Shade?" said the lead Zellat.

"Do?" said Shade, as though surprised that he should have to do anything at all.

"Yes, Lord."

"Let me face them," cried Caius suddenly stepping forward. "I'll take some of the Zellats. If they're coming from the north, they will have to pass the canyon to get to us. I can trap them there."

Shade thought for a while.

"Very well," he said at last. "Eighty shouldn't be too difficult to handle. Take a few hundred Zellats with you and take a few of the older stallions. You can sacrifice them first to soften the opposition up a bit before you move in for the kill."

"You heard the lord," said Caius immediately, addressing the Zellats. "Get them ready and choose some older stallions to send in first."

The Zellats nodded and marched Chub through the grass.

"Well, Caius," said Shade cheerfully when the Zellats had left. "This is a surprise."

"Do you think He sent them?" asked Caius.

"While he hides away?" said Shade. "It's possible, but I prefer to think that our assassin was not trained in vain. Well, we shall find out more when I've had time to question the prisoner. But just in case he tries anything, bring those two mares to me and double the guard around them and Gaia."

Caius bowed.

"If anyone tries to get to them, Caius, to rescue them, you have your orders. Kill them all."

"Gaia too?"

"All of them."

Again, Caius bowed.

"When you have defeated these upstarts," said Shade, send word and then stay where you are. It's time the herd was moving north again. This grassland is quite grazed out. I'll meet you by the canyon. And Caius, be sure to keep one or two of them alive, won't you? I want to question them too."

"Very good, Lord Shade," said Caius proudly and he turned and galloped off to join the gathering Zellats.

Shade stirred thoughtfully and looked out across the land at his army. His heart swelled.

"Arion," he whispered, "if you weren't just a fairy story I'd call you down from the skies to witness this. Those fools. They think you are the lord, but it is I who is the Lord of Violence."

Again Shade's eye ranged across the valley and suddenly began to laugh.

"Eighty, is that all you can send against me, Star?"

He paused and sucked in the warm air. At that moment Shade felt invincible.

Chapter 16

Tarn and his Band were moving swiftly now, restlessly scanning the terrain as they galloped, looking for the spot that Hulver had told them about, the place where they had agreed to wait for Misty and Ella. They were coming off the hills, close to late afternoon and the weather was even warmer than it had been the sun before, so their spirits were cheered a little by thoughts of long hot summers on the Prairie.

"It's so hot," muttered Blake, "for this time of year."

Armand, who was beside him, looked up at the sun before the glare made him turn his eyes away again.

No one had any answer as to what was happening to the sun now. Armand thought of Arion, but his comprehension could not carry him to the truth of it. For, hundreds of thousands of miles above them, the sun, which at the dawn of earth itself had stirred dead matter into life, was blistering and bubbling, spots of fire bursting at its edges, sending swords of flame miles high to cut the natural rhythm of the seasons. It was almost like the world itself was about to change.

The track the horses were following wound steeply down the hillside, which was sparsely wooded with sudden outcrops of scrubby trees, interspersed with rocks and enormous boulders. Lips of stone and rock overhangs provided panoramic vantage points over the land beneath. Below them, as they moved south, they could see a broad plain that stretched out from the base of the hillside they were on towards the undulating hills beyond. To the east was a forest, and to the west, more steep slopes, with a small river at the base of the foothills.

The path they were on tipped suddenly downwards, and as the horses got closer to the base of the hill, they saw a small lake at the bottom, feeding a stream that snaked away into the distance towards the far river. The water was dark blue-green, and the banks of the lake were strewn with rocks and rubble that time had torn away from the hill and cast at its feet. The lake was set well back, in a natural hollow and the sides stretched far away beyond the lake on either side, forming a pass straight ahead of them, no more than two tree lengths across, opening out to the Plain beyond.

"The canyon," whispered Tarn.

As they came to the water, their hooves skittered on the scree slopes, dislodging the loose rock. The dusty still air in the canyon began to echo with their sounds. Armand and Blake were the first to drink from the lake, and they found the water sweet and refreshing. Soon the others were collecting around it too, stirring the surface with their thirsty lips.

But Tarn looked up all the while and shook his head as his eyes ranged nervously around the place.

"Is anything wrong?" asked Armand.

"Yes," he answered gravely, "it gives plenty of cover and the water's sweet, but if we were ever caught here, we wouldn't stand a chance."

Armand looked keenly at Tarn.

"Perhaps we should go back up to the top of the slope. Height will give us an advantage and plenty of warning."

"No," said Tarn, "this is where we've agreed to meet Ella, and this is where we must wait. I only hope they hurry."

*****

As Tarn was talking to Armand, Ella and Misty were gazing down in horror at the great force that Shade had amassed. They had followed the Zellat's tracks right to the edge of the herd, and now the twins paused by a large rock as they wondered what to do. The day was closing, and Ella decided they should stay where they were until darkness and then steal among them. So they both grazed quietly, looking out nervously at the rows and rows of grazing stallions.

It was well after dark when they slipped off the hillside. They felt a sickening fear well up in their stomachs as they approached and came among them, but the horses were too preoccupied with other thoughts, and they hardly noticed the twins in the darkness.

"We should try to find the mares," whispered Ella as they went. "Try to find out more about Shade, if we can and if any of them have seen Chub."

Misty nodded to her sister.

On they went, passing row after row of horses. They felt the unnatural quietness of the place. A group of Zellats passed close by, but the twins dropped their heads to graze, and because they had drifted close to a clutch of mares, it looked as they were part of that group, and the Zellats moved on.

They pressed forward, and at last, they found themselves in the very centre of the huge herd, with females all around them. Again they pretended to graze in the darkness, but as they did so, they came close to a small Band of mares talking urgently together.

"Prophecy or no Prophecy," one mare was whispering gravely, "that's what I heard, and I believe it."

Ella began to move closer.

"But he came from our herd originally," said another.

"Yes," said the first mare. "But he died. Years ago. "Buffalo stampede I was told. What was left of him was probably picked and eaten by birds and wolves no doubt. What a way to die, horrible."

Ella's ears came up, and she looked at Misty.

"Then there's no hope," said another mare.

"There's always hope. Hey, you there. What are you doing?"

The mare that had done the most talking had spotted Ella and Misty. Ella realised there was nothing for it but to try and bluff it out. She lifted her head and trotted straight over to the mares. Misty took her lead and followed as calmly as she could.

"Well, what are you doing there?" asked the mare again.

"Nothing," answered Ella calmly. "We were just grazing."

"Why aren't you with your own?" said the mare. "You know it's forbidden to wonder after dark."

"I know," lied Ella and then she thought of what the mares had been saying about hope and the Prophecy. Ella decided to take a risk.

"But it's good to break the rules now and again, isn't it?" she whispered.

The mare looked at Ella suspiciously.

"Are you sure…" she asked coldly, "that you're not spies?"

Ella winced, but the other horses never saw it.

"Spies?" answered Ella calmly. "If you think that I'd spy for that scum, then perhaps you and I should take a walk and discuss it properly."

The mare looked carefully at Ella, and she didn't like the fire that flickered in her eye.

"All right," she said, "no need to get excited. If you can talk so openly about the Zellats, then you're free to graze near us."

Ella nodded.

"Tell me," she said, "where does Shade rest these days?"

"He is over there on the other side of the lake," gesturing the direction with her head. "Why?"

"No reason. Except that one day, I should like to tell him what I really think of him."

"And it would be your last day," said the mare, smiling, "if you could get anywhere near him."

"What do you mean?"

"You know they never let anyone through. He's guarded day and night by at least twenty Zellats, even when he travels through the herd. They even have a guard around Gaia."

Ella looked up.

"Gaia?" she said.

"That's right."

"Poor Gaia," said Ella. "They say her only friends are the four mares that returned years ago."

"Two, you mean," said the mare looking oddly at Ella.

"What's your name? I've never seen you around here before."

"Err, no…" stammered Ella. "My sister and I…, we only came in seven suns ago."

"Then how do you know of Gaia?" asked the mare carefully.

"Oh, the others are always talking about her and her friends."

The mare looked over at Misty, and when she saw her, she looked back at Ella and pawed the ground.

"You're twins," she said with surprise. "The spitting image."

"That's right," said Ella.

"It's odd that I haven't seen you around before. You stand out enough."

"We like to keep ourselves to ourselves," said Ella quickly. "Not all the mares feel as we do about Shade."

Her words seemed to reassure the mare.

"No, no indeed," she muttered in the dark, "and if I were you, I wouldn't talk so openly about it. But you'll soon learn."

"Gaia's friends," said Ella, ignoring the warning. "Now what are they called again.

"Aiko and Rosa."

"That's right," said Ella casually but feeling a sudden weakness in her legs. "Aiko and Rosa. I'd like to meet them one day."

"No chance of that."

"Why not?"

"They always used to keep them separate, under constant guard. Then this morning, when they brought the prisoner in, they put them both with Gaia."

Both Ella and Misty's heads had come up, and they were listening intently.

"Of course," said Ella, "the prisoner. Where are they keeping him?"

"You do ask a lot of questions," said the mare, growing suspicious again. "Over there, by the cottonwood tree."

"Ah, yes," said Ella, her eyes glinting. "Well, we'd better be getting back."

The mare shrugged, but as Ella and Misty set off in the direction of the cottonwood tree, Ella suddenly turned and called to her.

"But he didn't die, you know."

"Who?" said the startled mare.

"The One. The one who fled from the herd. He's still alive, I've seen him myself."

All the little group of mares heard it, and as Ella and Misty vanished into the night, the mares looked at each other in amazement.

"That was close," whispered Misty as they ran. "I thought for a moment we were lost."

"I know," said Ella. "But did you hear?"

"Mother?" said Misty.

"Yes. And Luna. What could have happened to them?"

"Perhaps they escaped when we did," said Misty. "Luna never really wanted to come back."

"No," agreed Ella, but her heart was deeply troubled. As the twins went through the darkness, a breeze came up, and they noticed that a mist was settling around the herd, drifting up in wisps across the grass. It grew thicker as they neared the cottonwood tree, which was set apart from the edge of a larger wood. They stopped as they spotted a group of Zellat guards through the fog. There were five of them, four feeding in a semi-circle near the tree and one on his own, patrolling up and down. Nearby, was Chub.

Although they were still a good way off and it was quite dark, Misty recognised him immediately and winced as she saw the cuts and bruises on his side and face.

"Chub," she gasped.

"Hush, Misty, they'll hear us," said Ella. "We must try to think of something."

"Misty looked hard at her sister.

"But Ella, you know what Tarn said. We've found out where they're keeping him and something of Shade. Shouldn't we…"

"We're here now," said Ella smiling, "so it's our duty to try to rescue him."

Misty's eyes opened wider, but she didn't argue, for she was suddenly desperate for Chub. So, in the darkness, the twins backed into the trees at the edge of the wood by a large clump of bushes and began to whisper together. After a while, they had formed a sort of plan. It was a terrible risk, and the two stared at each other fearfully when they hit on it.

"We'll have to trust to darkness and the fog to work it," said Ella, dropping her muzzle and scooping up some earth and rubbing some of it against Misty's face.

"That's better," she said when she had finished. "Now not even Arion could tell us apart. If we get separated, we'll meet by the rock."

"Right," Misty nodded. "Who'll go first?"

"I will," said Ella.

"No, I will," said Misty suddenly.

Before Ella could argue, Misty had turned and sprung off towards the Zellats. Ella waited nervously for a while and then followed her sister into the fog.

Misty ran straight ahead, her head raised and her tail twitching. When she was about a tree length away, she started to graze as she drifted closer and closer towards the lone guard patrolling, while the other guards talked quietly in the night. The guard didn't see her at first, but after a while he heard a sound and looked up, his eyes trying to pierce the deepening mist.

"Who's there?" he said.

Misty didn't answer.

At first, the guard thought he must be mistaken but then a gust of wind cleared the fog for an instant, and he saw Misty standing there, staring back at him.

"You there," he called gruffly. "What are you doing here?"

Misty tilted her head quizzically and then whispered in a strange voice. "Don't be afraid, I won't hurt you."

The guard was almost too startled to answer.

"Hurt me?" he said in amazement. "A mare hurt a Zellat guard?"

"Not just any mare," answered Misty as gravely as she could.

"What do you mean? said the guard. "Who are you? What do you want?"

"Arion sent me," said Misty and just as she did so another bank of fog rolled in around her. This time, she jumped to the side and skirted a little way around the guard.

"Stand still," said the guard angrily. "You know it is forbidden to mention that name."

"Forbidden?" whispered Misty. "Who could forbid it?"

"Lord Shade," said the guard. "And when I-"

"Peace," said Misty. "Arion has a message for you. He wants you to know-"

"Silence," said the guard even more furiously. "What nonsense are you talking?"

"Don't you believe in me?" whispered Misty. "In Arion?"

Again, the fog closed on Misty, and she darted around the guard. This time, she didn't wait for him to address her before speaking.

"Here I am," she whispered, "all around you."

"Stand still, I say," snorted the guard, swinging round. "Stop playing games."

Misty's face was clearly visible again, and she held the guard's gaze coldly.

"Games?" she answered. "This is no game. The Zellats cruelty is no game. Why are you torturing your kind?"

The guard was about to lunge at Misty when she backed into the fog.

"Hey, come back," he said, but just at that moment, another voice came through the night, right behind him. When the guard turned, he was amazed to see Misty's face, or what he thought was Misty's face, still gazing at him through the fog. It was impossible that the mare could have run around him that fast.

"I'm still here," said Ella, imitating Misty's voice as best she could.

"But…How…?" stammered the guard, as Ella backed into the fog herself vanishing.

"Because I am all around you," said Misty from behind the guard, "in the trees, in your dreams and worst of all, your nightmares."

Again the guard turned, and there was a mare, back in the spot where she had been speaking before. The guard could hardly believe his eyes. He stamped the ground and shook his head. He thought he was dreaming. The fog had once more swathed Misty in mystery as she whispered through the night.

"Fear me…"

"…For I come when you least expect it," Ella went on reappearing to the left of the guard. He was really shaken by now and kept swinging back and forth as the twins played their game of voices.

"I need some sleep," muttered the guard to himself and Ella and Misty fell silent.

"Hey, Drago, what's up," said another stallion suddenly through the darkness. "I thought I heard voices."

It was the guard's commander, who had been resting earlier and had brought another Zellat with him to check on the patrol.

"Nothing sir," answered Drago, still bewildered by the twins' trick.

"What do you mean nothing? You were talking to someone."

The guard started to stammer.

"There was a mare over there… or at least over there… but…"

"What's wrong with you?" snorted the commander angrily. "Make sense."

"She said she was Arion," whispered the guard in a voice that was beginning to tremble, "and that she was everywhere."

Yet something about the eerie cloud unsettled him, for they were nervous with the upcoming trek and their own nights work with Chub had filled their hearts with darkness.

"Rubbish," he squealed. "There's no one out there at all."

"She came from there," said the guard, "but in an instant, she was behind me again."

"Drago, have you lost your wits?" snapped the commander. "You'll pay for this in the morning."

"You must not punish him for telling the truth," came a still calm voice out of the fog. The commander looked up, and now he caught sight of Misty too.

"Who are you!" shouted the commander, as she backed away.

"Arion," said Ella from the right, emerging from the fog for just a moment.

The commander and the other Zellat looked at Drago in amazement.

"Catch her," he shouted.

"Which way?" said Drago.

"Over here," cried Misty.

"No, over here," shouted Ella.

The three Zellats hesitated, looking left and right and they leapt forward towards the spot where Ella's voice had come from. They plunged into the mist, and as they did so, they caught sight of the mare's silhouette racing for the trees.

Ella galloped as fast as she could and found a hiding place where she could observe the confused stallions.

The guards were too startled to think clearly, and they ran on blindly in the darkness, blundering straight past Ella as they did so. The mare waited for a few moments through the fog as she caught sight of a shape in front of her. Misty had joined her.

They're falling for it," said Ella.

"Thank Arion."

The mist was thinning again now, and the twins could see the two remaining Zellats by the tree and Chub nearby. The guards had heard the commotion and were looking around wearily.

"But there's no time," said Ella. "The others will give up soon enough."

"Then we must hurry," urged Misty and she sprang forward. Ella gasped as her sister ran straight up to the guard on the right. He swung round as he saw her coming out of the mist, but as quick as lightening, Misty turned and gave him an angry kick before galloping away again, back into the fog.

The guard paused in astonishment, turning to his comrade.

"Watch the prisoner," he grunted. "I'm going to teach that mare a lesson she'll never forget."

The last remaining guard moved closer to Chub, gazing around in confusion as Ella stepped out of the fog a good way away from where Misty had vanished.

"What the?" said the confused guard.

"Ghosts," cried Ella, loud enough to attract Chub's attention. Chub was almost as amazed as the guard but lost no time.

"Stand there," snorted the guard to Ella, as he fronted her aggressively as she approached.

"You can do nothing to a ghost," cried Ella as she walked at him.

"We'll see about that," said the guard.

He never noticed Chub behind him He felt it first across his haunch as Chub brought his hooves down hard. But as he swung round in pain, Chub struck again, this time knocking him clean off balance. As he fell, Ella lashed out furiously with her hind legs. The blow hit the Zellat straight in the face, and he was thrown sideways.

"Come on, Chub," she cried.

Ella was already galloping, and Chub didn't argue. Tired and injured as he was, he raced after her into the mist. The guard on the ground was too dazed and confused even to know what was happening.

They ran and ran along the edge of the wood and now night, and the fog came to their rescue for none of the herd spotted them. After a while, they rose up the hill, and Ella caught sight of the rock where they had agreed to meet Misty if they got separated.

"We'll wait here, Chub," she panted as they came to a halt. "I hope she got away."

They weren't long in waiting. They soon heard a horse coming towards them through the darkness. It was Misty, and she was alone.

"Thank Arion," cried Ella delightedly.

I had a difficult time to shake off that light foot," said Misty, smiling at Chub.

The sisters stared at each other, and suddenly they both burst out laughing.

"If it's that easy," said Misty, beaming, "maybe there's some hope after all."

"Come on, then," said Ella when they calmed down a little. "We'd better get back to Tarn and the others. They'll be waiting, and we've seen enough here. We've even got a little surprise for them," she added, smiling at Chub. "I only wish we'd been able to find out about Fauna."

As she said it, Misty saw the look on Chub's face.

"Chub, what is it?" she asked. "What's wrong?"

Chub dropped his eyes.

"Chub, you know something, tell us."

Chub gazed helplessly at the twins.

"I'm sorry," he whispered, "but they died, Luna and your mother, Fauna. Together, on the v-v-very day of our escape."

Ella and Misty stood side by side and lowered their heads. Their joy and exhilaration at rescuing Chub had turned into despair. When Ella raised her eyes to Chub again, they were burning with anger.

"Come then," she said. "The quicker we get back to the others the quicker we'll have our revenge."

"How far away are they?" said Chub quietly.

"Not too far," answered Ella. "they're waiting for us at the canyon."

"The canyon?" cried Chub in horror. "But that's where the Zellats are heading now."

"Then they know about the others," gasped Ella.

"Yes, they saw us all on the hill. Before they captured me."

"How many are there?"

"Over a hundred and fifty, maybe more."

"Then we can still beat them there, cried, Ella. "But there's no time to lose."

Chapter 17

Tarn pawed the earth restlessly. The night had been fitful and the day's wait even worse, for as he examined the terrain he had grown more and more unhappy with the meeting place. He was frantically worried about Ella too and kept scolding himself for ever having let the twins go.

The young horse suddenly started. Bits of stone and rock were skittering down the side of the slopes. As he and the others looked up, they could see nothing above them. But now Armand cried out. Stallions were coming straight towards them through the pass.

"Quick," cried Tarn, but as he said it one of the stallions called out. He was looking up at the high slopes again. There above them, others horses appeared, fanning out across the hilltop. Hundreds of them.

"Hurry," shouted Tarn, his voice reverberating through the canyon. "Form up."

They didn't need to be told twice. Tarn's group of eighty came together in the stone hollow, their backs to the lake, one group turned to the walls of the mountain and the others led by Tarn, faced towards the pass.

"What do we do now?" cried Armand frantically.

"We fight," answered Tarn. "But let them come to us. If they charge, you and Blake take some of our stallions to the right and left of them and hit them from the sides."

Blake and Armand nodded and turned to face the oncoming Zellats. Instead of charging, however, the enemy waited, just beyond the entrance of the canyon.

A silence descended, and suddenly a voice rang out from the heights above them.

"You are surrounded. There is no escape," cried the lone stallion.

"What do you want from us?" shouted Tarn angrily.

"Nothing but your servitude," cried the stallion, "or your lives. But first I want to know if He is among you. The one of the Prophecy."

"Star," whispered Armand.

"Who dares ask?" cried Tarn, stamping his hooves defiantly.

"My name is Caius. I demand to know, in the name of Lord Shade."

"You can tell your master," cried Tarn contemptuously, "that He, is not with us, but that we have returned to free our kind from Shade's tyranny and restore faith in Arion's way."

"There is no such way, only Shade's way."

Caius suddenly stopped. He spied something below him.

"So," he called out, "Blake, you are here too? With some of your traitors I see. Aren't you a little old for such foolishness?"

"Come down here, Caius," he shouted angrily, "and I will show you how I can fight."

Caius smiled. He wouldn't have dreamed of doing anything of the kind.

"Blake," he answered, "the privilege of age and power is that others do the fighting for you if you know how to rule. Leonardo never understood that.

Morro had more chance of doing so, but he chose to follow your idiotic instincts. This is why he lives by our great herd, the object of our pleasure and blind as his beliefs."

"Lives?" he gasped.

"But enough," Caius went on. "It is time."

Caius suddenly let out a loud squealing sound, and on cue, some of the Zellats on the slopes around him began to descend towards Tarn as his group. Several stallions ran out to meet them, but now the Zellats in the pass were charging towards them.

Tarn cried out, "come on."

Tarn, Armand, Blake and about twenty stallions raced forward to meet them. Blake and Armand split right and left, and suddenly the canyon was filled with the clatter of hooves and the noise and grunts of fighting stallions. But the fight stopped again almost as soon as it had started. Armand rushed into the fray, rearing in front of a stallion when he realised the enemy was fleeing from them back to the pass entrance.

"After them," he cried delightedly to the others and was about to rush after them when Tarn called him back.

"Stop, it's a trick. That's what they want you to do."

Armand pulled up, and Tarn led them back to the lake where the other stallions were holding off the assault on their flank. The enemy was randomly probing for a weakness, and each time the Zellats from the canyon pass surged forward they would fight only briefly and then retreat again, trying to draw Tarn and his Band out of position.

Armand and Blake led each sally, and soon their hooves were red with blood, and several from both sides lay dead or dying around them. Armand's leg was bleeding, but none of the remaining horses seemed badly hurt. Armand grew more confident, but Tarn looked back at him gravely, for it was the fifth time the enemy had surged towards them, and he realised what Caius was doing. He was slowly sapping them of strength.

Blake and Armand were exhausted with the efforts. It was growing dark in the canyon too, the evening draining the colour from the lake and turning the stallions to shadows among the broken stones. But still they fought on, as the stars pricked through the night.

"Do you think we can hold them?" cried Blake as he and Tarn met by the water's edge.

Tarn pawed the earth. "They're trying to tire us out. That's what Caius wants. He seems to have kept a large force in reserve. When he sends those in, who knows what will happen. Our best bet is to make a run for it. If we can break through the pass, we might have a chance."

But as he said it there was a loud sound from above them. They looked round and realised that the Zellats were disengaging.

There was still enough light to see the pass and Blake shuddered as he realised that the horses in the pass were pulling back. Then, through the middle of the pass and the bleeding ranks of retreating horses, came the second wave, fresh and mean.

A hundred Zellats were advancing in line, with purpose and confidence. Tarn and his embattled Band looked on nervously.

"Come on," cried one of the stallions suddenly. "We're not afraid of you. Who's with me?"

It was Armand.

"I'm with you Armand," cried Blake, running up to him.

Tarn was with them in an instant.

"We must try and break them in the centre," cried Tarn desperately.

Tarn could see that the Zellats had stopped now and were waiting in their neat lines. Forty of them had come ahead of the others and were stamping the ground.

"It looks like they're going to attack in groups, like the previous tactic," said Tarn. "Well, first we must test their strength. We'll split into two. Blake and I will lead one and Armand, you lead the other. It doesn't matter which attacks first."

"I'll go," said Armand immediately.

"Very well. Test them as they did to us earlier," said Tarn, "and Armand, when I call, pull away quickly."

Armand nodded gravely, and with forty stallions at his back, he led them forward. Tarn and Blake watched as their friend approached the pass. When they were a tree length away from the front line, the Zellats suddenly surged forward. Horses were rearing, kicking and biting. The two groups became one.

In the dust and melee Tarn could barely see Armand but as he looked on it was becoming obvious that the Zellats were too strong for his exhausted troop.

"No," he cried as he saw a stallion fall, then another.

"Call them back," cried Blake.

Tarn rushed forward. He called out furiously but if he had even heard him there was little Armand could do, for the Zellats were clearly overpowering them.

"We've got to help them," cried Blake.

"Come on then," shouted Tarn.

The second group rushed forward to help Armand but as they did so a shrill sound went out, and the stallion reared on his back legs.

"Pull out." he cried.

"It was Armand.

The others had heard him and did their best to disengage, kicking furiously with their hind legs to get away. The Zellats seemed to have no desire to pursue them, and suddenly Armand was galloping back towards the lake, followed by those who had survived. Only twenty of them did so.

"It's hopeless," cried Armand as he ran up. His neck was badly bloodied. "They're far too strong for us."

Tarn nodded.

"We'll never make it through the pass," said Blake. "What can we do?"

Tarn shook his head.

"We can't make it up those steep slopes behind us that's for sure," he said quietly.

"Then we're lost," whispered Armand.

The survivors were silent as they stood in the canyon. Their hearts as tired as their weak bodies.

"Very well then," said Tarn after a while. "We shall just have to try to make it through the pass. If only one of us survives, perhaps he can get to Shade."

With that, there was a great shudder of noise across the grass. The Zellats - all of them now - were advancing, lined again in rows. Tarn's beleaguered Band turned to face them, their legs trembling with fear and exhaustion.

But when they were still quite a way away, to Tarn's surprise they suddenly stopped.

"What is it?" whispered Blake.

"Listen," said Armand.

Above them, from the top of the canyon slopes, there was a thunderous noise of hooves. Rocks and boulders were showering down the slopes, a waterfall of stones splashing into the still pool. Then, to the friends' amazement, stallions began to emerge from the shadows, leaping onto the grass and rushing towards them.

"Prepare yourselves, cried Armand furiously.

"Wait," shouted Blake, "look."

"Ella," cried Tarn delightedly. "It's Ella and Misty. And look who's with them," said Armand.

The friends' amazement could hardly have been greater for at the twins' side now came not only Chub but Nacho too. The fear that had gripped the Band was instantly transformed as the incoming stallions greeted them.

"I don't know how you worked this magic," cried Tarn as Ella ran up to him, "but I'm glad-"

"Don't say it," said Ella. "We rescued Chub, as you can see, but then we heard you were in danger and were rushing back to warn you when we met Nacho here. You'd better listen to what he's got to say."

"Arion be with you," panted Nacho. "I'm sorry we couldn't get through sooner. We weren't sure how many there were."

"But I thought..." Armand started to say.

"We've been tracking you for days," Nacho went on, "and by the look of it, we've arrived just in time.

"Yes," said Tarn. "How many of you are there?"

"Just over a hundred."

"With us, that makes around one hundred and sixty then. Caius can't have more than that. So maybe we've got a chance if we can survive the night."

Nacho peered through the darkness, back towards the pass and though he could see them only dimly, he realised that the Zellats were retreating again.

"Tomorrow we can try to break through," said Tarn.

"And by then there may be more of us," added Nacho.

"More, but how?"

"Star."

"Star," cried Armand delightedly and Tarn gazed at Ella in wonder. She was smiling.

"After you left," Nacho went on, "Star spoke to those that had remained loyal to him. He has sent word out across the land that the Prophecy is true."

"But where is he?" said Tarn.

"I don't know."

Tarn looked gravely at Ella.

"Well if he does eventually decide to come, it may be too late," said Tarn quietly.

The horses stirred around him. Though the air was chill in the hollow of night and many of them were severely wounded, talk of Star and the Prophecy, the reappearance of Chub and the twins, not to mention the sudden increase in their numbers, had lifted their spirits beyond measure. Hope was stirring once again.

Suddenly they heard a voice from up high that echoed angrily across the canyon.

"You down there," cried Caius in the darkness. "Listen to me. To resist is useless. You have new friends now, and perhaps you think you can escape. But you can't. If you surrender now, I give you my word that none of you will be harmed."

"Caius," answered Tarn, instantly and angrily, letting his voice range through the blackness, "save your lies. We will never surrender to you. But there are enough of us now to fight you and others are on their way."

"Indeed," answered Caius coldly, though there was some faint note of uncertainty in his voice. "But I don't need to fight you, and you will never make it through the pass alive."

Meanwhile, Lord Shade will shortly bring his whole army through here and then what can you do? Die. I can simply hold you trapped here until then."

"Then do your worst," shouted Tarn.

But Caius had definitely unsettled them all.

"Very well," whispered Tarn. "Until the morning then."

*****

The distant stars shone down from the cold heavens as Shade's colossal herd waited for dawn to break and for daylight to herald their continued journey north.

After so many moons the land here was grazed out, and they were all expectant and restless. But something else was stirring through their ranks in the darkness. News had just reached them of the battle at the canyon, together with the strange rumour of more horses coming from the north.

Contingents of Zellats were moving amongst the herd, checking and making sure that everyone had their orders for the next day's exodus. It had been very carefully planned, and Shade had given instructions that they should make straight for the canyon as fast as they could. But something else had made their leader especially vigilant. In the late hours of darkness Caius and ten Zellats had returned to the herd. Caius had been running hard and asked to be shown into Shade's presence.

"What's wrong?" said one of the Zellats to the commander as they paced the herd in darkness.

"Who knows?"

"Whatever it is it won't please Shade. He's still angry that the prisoner escaped."

"We'd better watch it tonight then. What have you heard?"

"Some sort of skirmish. We've got them pinned down, though."

"So there'll be some fighting."

The commander shrugged.

"A bit of mopping up. I doubt you'll get to see any of it. You'll have to get your kicks somewhere else. Go and take your frustrations out on blind Morro again."

"I suppose so. Though there'll be enough to think about when we move."

"True enough," agreed the commander, "especially with all these humans around. We've lost a good number of our stragglers to those men."

"Serves them right for straying," snorted the Zellat. "That will teach them the meaning of discipline."

"It's a bit late for them to learn anything now," chuckled the commander.

Both of them laughed. Their party had come to a copse of cottonwood trees that ran a little way along the edge of a meadow above the lake, where many of the younger horses had settled. The commander of a group of Zellats went ahead of the others, and they pulled up suddenly. He had heard something through the copse, where the trees suddenly thinned out. It was a pair of young colts, whispering in the darkness.

"But it was just a silly dream," one was saying.

"No, I heard him clearly," said the other.

"But you said you'd been dozing."

Yes, but it was just as I was waking up. The voice came through the trees. As clearly as I'm talking to you now."

"And?"

"And it told me to listen."

"Didn't you go and see who it was?"

"I didn't care to," answered the colt. "Besides, I was half asleep."

"There you are, then."

"No, it wasn't my dream," insisted the colt, "it was in the wood."

"And didn't you ask who was there?" said the other colt gravely.

"Of course I did."

"Well?"

At this, the young colt's voice dropped to almost an inaudible whisper.

"The voice, it said this. "I am He who you have betrayed. And I am you. I am…"

The colt paused.

"Well?" whispered the other colt.

"Arion."

The listening Zellats looked at each other in amazement, but the commander shook his head.

"Is that all?"

"No, I went on talking to him. What do you want of me? I said."

"For you to heal yourself," came the voice.

"But how? I asked."

"By carrying out my lore. You are what you are. Shade can never change that."

Again the Zellats stirred but still the commander held them back.

"But what should I do? I said."

"Look for me," came the voice, "for I have come to free you all. To fulfil the Prophecy."

"The Prophecy, that's what he said."

"Do you know the Prophecy?" said the other colt.

"I heard something when I was young."

"What else did the voice say?"

"Nothing. After that, there was nothing, just the wind in the trees. I called out. Wait, tell me more. But nothing came back. I ran towards the place I'd heard it…"

"Well?"

"Well, this is the really strange thing. The trees were very widely spaced, and there was a clearing. But there was no one there at all. No one."

"But it was dark. Maybe someone was playing tricks on you."

"There was definitely something there."

Beyond the trees, the Zellats looked wonderingly at their commander.

"Shall we take them?" whispered the stallion who had been addressing him earlier.

"No," he whispered back, "We don't want any troubles with the mares, so close to the trek. But if there's any fighting to be done tomorrow, make sure they're at the front of it."

"What do you think it means?" said the Zellat as the commander led them through the night.

"Just foolish talk," he answered. "I've been hearing such nonsense more and more of late. It must be because of the trek. Everyone's nervous."

The Zellats ran on until they came to the top of a wide meadow by a larger forest. Here the ground was badly scarred, for this was the place that many of the Zellats came to train and mock fight, even at this time there were some testing their strength, they never rested.

The commander moved through the ranks, nodding his head approvingly at the sight of his Zellats. They were at their peak of fitness, and many were now spoiling for a real fight.

Well, let's hope there are some of these 'outcasts' left to fight, thought the commander to himself as he walked.

He reached a group of young stallions, training to become Zellats. As he passed by, one of them looked up and nudged the other next to him.

"Hey," he whispered excitedly, "that was a commander."

"What do you know about it?" said another next to him scornfully.

"I know I saw him training some of the Zellats yesterday."

"Well, what of it?"

"I'm going to be a commander one day," said the young stallion.

"You'll never make a commander," snorted one.

"Oh, yes I will. When I grow up, I'll show you."

"No, you won't. You'll never make a Zellat your too small."

The young stallion lifted his head angrily.

"Say that again," he snorted, coming forwards in the night.

"I said you're a weakling."

The second horse came forward, and the two of them stood to face each other staring and posturing.

Suddenly, they both pulled back and dropped their heads guiltily. A stallion was standing behind them in the darkness.

He must have been seven years old, and he stood strong and proud. They couldn't make out his face in the blackness but assumed he was a Zellat.

"Why are you fighting?" asked the stallion quietly.

The youngsters glared at each other, slightly puzzled by the question.

"He said I'd never make a commander," said the first sulkily.

"And he won't. You need to be able to fight, and you need strength and courage, don't you? That's why you're a Zellat, isn't it?"

"Tell me," he went on softly, "do you like fighting?"

Again the young horses looked at each other, surprised.

"But that's what the Zellats do, they fight. That's why all animal kind fears us. That's why we are greater than everyone else. That's what Shade tells us."

In the darkness the young horse fancied he caught a furious glint in the stallion's eye.

"And you want to kill things, do you?" said the horse gently.

"Oh, yes, when I am old enough."

The stallion shook his head.

"And do you think that this is what Arion wants of you?" he whispered in the night.

"Who?" said the youngster.

"Arion. When I was your age," the stallion said, smiling as he addressed all the youngsters, "I found many better things to do than fight, you know. We'd play from sun up to sun down and listen to the stories of old, of Arion and many other adventures."

"Play?" said one of the youngsters with interest.

"Oh, yes," said the stallion. "But I suppose Shade has changed all that."

"You must call him Lord Shade."

"I'll do nothing of the kind," answered the stallion.

Now the youngsters looked at each other, and there was fear in their eyes.

"I'll tell on you," said one of the youngsters.

"Come now," answered the stallion without anger. "That isn't very brave, is it?"

The youngster looked down guiltily.

"But if you really want to tell the Zellats, why don't you say that there is a stallion amongst the herd that thinks Shade is nothing more than a lying light-foot and the Zellats are no better than vermin."

The youngsters shuddered.

"Tell them their days are numbered and that you all will run free again on the vast Prairies and play together just as you should."

With that the great stallion turned and vanished into the night, leaving the younglings in stunned silence.

A wind had come up, and above their heads the clouds were skittering through the sky, breaking the surface of the heavens and fretting the canopy of stars with ribbons of darkness.

Chapter 18

On the edge of the great herd, an old mare was looking up through the veil of night, gazing at the twinkling specks of light that spattered the sky above her. They had no meaning for her, except in the tales told to her as a filly. Tales of Arion, a Prophecy. As her eyes ranged the heavens, they came upon two stars that were close together and brighter than the rest, and suddenly the mare's heart tightened in anguish.

"Abrazo," she whispered, "you are up there, aren't you? With my little Star. You're looking after each other."

Gaia shook her head and looked around. There were Zellats all about her, but the guards had been told to stand off in a wide ring. Two other mares were coming towards her. Both were slightly younger than Gaia. It was Aiko and Rosa.

"How are you, my dear?" said Rosa as the two mares came up.

Gaia smiled.

"Well enough. But I was thinking about them."

Rosa nodded.

"Poor Gaia," she said. "I think about Chub all the time."

"And I about Armand," sighed Aiko.

"Look at us," said Gaia sadly. "Three old mares lost in the world, with nothing but our memories to feed on."

"At least we're together, my dear," said Rosa.

"Yes, and at least your little ones are alive and free, although they won't be so little anymore." Gaia smiled at her friends.

"Yes, I often wonder how they've grown," pondered Rosa.

"Why do you think Shade still wants to keep us here?" said Aiko suddenly.

Gaia looked strangely at her friend. She had never told the other two the real reason why she stayed with Shade was to protect them. But she too wondered why Shade had suddenly doubled the guard over all three of them.

"I heard a few of the Zellats talking," said Aiko. "There's been fighting nearby. Maybe it's got something to do with that."

"Fighting?" said Gaia with surprise.

"Yes," said Aiko, "they mentioned that they were challenged by horses that had come from the north."

"They won't survive for long when the rest of Shade's army move forward in the morning. Nobody's going to stop him now."

Gaia's head dropped, her shoulders sagged, and her face betrayed a loss of hope.

Rosa and Aiko looked at one another then tried to comfort Gaia.

"As long as we are all together and as long as our children are out there free, there is always hope, Gaia. We mustn't give up."

Gaia nodded half-heartedly agreeing with her friends. Gaia wandered away, under the watchful eye of a few Zellat guards. She rested in the grass and sighed as she looked into the darkness.

Aiko's mention of the fight had stirred something in her, and that seeming act of defiance brought back her thoughts of Abrazo. She could see his confident features in her mind's eye, his strong face and coat shining in the sunlight. She could almost hear his assuring, gentle voice and smell his scent. Gaia closed her eyes. Abrazo was gone forever, murdered that night on the hill. That terrible night when she gave birth to Star, her little treasure whose life she had tried to save, only to have it snatched away by Arion. Gaia suddenly felt desperately old and bitterly alone. She began to doze again, and in the dreams that stole over her thoughts, she was troubled.

Gaia suddenly woke. It was pitch black, and the stars had been blanked out by thick clouds. A breeze was murmuring through the nearby trees and rustling through the grass. Gaia stirred. A stallion was coming towards her. She could see the outline of his shape as he approached. He was walking slowly, but in the darkness, she could not tell which of the guards it was.

"What are you doing here?" she snapped as the stallion drew nearer. "You know Shade does not allow you to approach unless I call."

The stallion stopped but said nothing.

"Well," Gaia went on, "answer me. Why are you disturbing my sleep?"

The stallion lifted his head.

"Answer me," she insisted.

"Mother," the stallion whispered through the darkness.

Gaia looked up in amazement.

"What did you say?"

"Mother," whispered the stallion again.

Gaia's heart trembled.

"Mother, it's me, Star."

Gaia's legs began to shiver. The stallion was by her side now, and as Gaia blinked fearfully up at him in the darkness, she felt as if her heart would burst with joy. She looked hard at him, trying to take it all in.

"But it can't be. You can't…"

"It can, Mother," said Star quietly. "I am alive and have returned to fulfil the Prophecy."

Gaia blinked back at him, but as she looked into those eyes and caught his scent, she knew immediately that it was true. Her little Star had come back to her.

"Star, it's really you? My, you've grown into a fine stallion." Gaia nuzzled him warmly.

"Yes, Mother," smiled Star, "I'm sorry it has been so long. But I never knew."

Gaia gazed in wonderment, not wanting this dream to end. She blinked her eyes hard. He was still standing there in front of her, his form as real as her unbounded happiness.

"But how, Star, how?" she said at last.

"There is no time," said Star quietly. "I will explain everything once my work is completed."

"But what are you doing here?" gasped Gaia, suddenly fearful and looking around towards the Zellat guard. "It's not safe."

"I've come to face Shade," said Star, "and end his tyranny."

"No, no you mustn't," cried Gaia. "We must get you away," she replied in a nervous whisper.

"The time for flight is long gone," answered Star with a strength she had not heard before. "I must face Shade, and I need your help."

"No, I will not lose you again," pleaded Gaia.

In an instant, she realised that her Star was in terrible danger and suddenly the part of the Prophecy that had haunted her for so long flashed through her head.

"Sacrifice shall be his meaning…"

"No," she gasped, I will not let you throw your life away, you mustn't."

"If Arion wishes this of me, Mother, I would gladly give myself to free us all. I cannot escape my destiny."

"There must be another way."

As Gaia looked at him, standing there so boldly in the night, she suddenly fell silent. Now the amazement of seeing her young colt, all grown up, was giving way to silent awe.

"If Arion wills it," she murmured.

"We must hurry," said Star. "My friends are in danger. Chub, Armand, Ella, Misty and Tarn are caught in a nearby canyon."

"Chub and Armand?"

"Yes, I've got to help them somehow. But first, I must meet Shade, face to face."

"But why?" said Gaia in a desperate whisper. "have you come to kill him?"

Star shook his head.

"No," he said quietly, "not yet. If I am to free everyone from Shade's lies, then his death alone will not suffice. They must all witness a stronger sign. But first I want Shade to know that I am here."

"But he will have you killed," said Gaia.

"Not if I get him alone," said Star. "And there you can help me."

Gaia nodded.

"But, Mother, as soon as you have shown me to him," said Star gravely, "you must get safely away from here. That is also why I came, to help you to escape."

"Aiko and Rosa are with me," said Gaia, looking over to the two mares who were some way away. "I won't go without them."

"Good," said Star, delighted that the mares were still alive, "that is very good. But choose your moment wisely. Try not to alert suspicion. Now, where is Shade?"

Gaia looked into the night.

"I don't know. Inspecting the herd."

"You must call him, Mother," said Star "and somehow get the guards away so that I can speak with him alone. Then you must all go into the hills until it's over."

Again Gaia looked fearfully at Star.

"Are you certain this is what you want?" she said.

"I have no choice," answered Star quietly. "I wanted to live as a free Mustang of the Plains, but how could I or any of the others be free when there are so many crying in pain? The things I have seen, Mother."

Gaia stared gravely at her son. He had grown beyond her comprehension, and as she gazed at his aged face, she reflected on those times long ago when he had started his journey, and she marvelled.

"There is so much of your father in you."

Gaia nodded and walked nearer to the ring of Zellats. The guards were completely unaware of the stranger that had crept through their ranks in the night.

"You," cried Gaia to one of them.

The Zellat, who had been caught napping, turned to face Gaia.

"I want to see Lord Shade."

Star could not hear any more. He had drawn back into the cover of nearby trees. He watched Gaia as she gave instructions to the guard and though his thoughts were consumed with the coming battle and of what Arion wanted of him, now he silently gave thanks for having given him the chance to see her again and to have kept her alive. He gazed away towards Aiko and Rosa and wondered what they would make of Armand and Chub too.

Gaia padded back towards Star.

"It's done," she whispered.

"Good, now go and wake the others and get them ready. And, Mother, do not hesitate. I will find you."

She nodded.

As the Zellat guard raced away to find Shade, his master was not inspecting the herd as Gaia had imagined. He had finished consulting with Caius.

Shade was resting, twitching. His dreams troubled him. A great moon hung above him in the sky, lighting up the nearby trees and the hard earth. Then suddenly a horse was coming towards him. His head was lowered, and as Shade looked on in amazement, it seemed to him that the stallion's body was glowing, shimmering in the pale wash of the distant moon.

"Who are you?" whispered Shade fearfully in his sleep.

"What do you want?"

The stallion stopped and then raised his head. Shade pulled back in horror as he saw his face, scarred and mangled and covered in blood.

"Abrazo?" he gasped.

Abrazo stood before him in that ghostly light, the stallion's dead eyes looking coldly down on him.

"Abrazo, it isn't you," hissed Shade. "You're dead. We killed you."

Very slowly the stallion began to shake his head.

"What do you want of me?" said Shade, shivering in his sleep. "What have you come to tell me?"

Still, the apparition said nothing.

"Speak to me, damn you!" cried Shade. "Speak!"

But with that, the stallion turned his bloodied head and walked slowly away. The moon seemed to go out suddenly, and Shade screamed. The old stallion gasped and opened his eye. His body was drenched in sweat.

"Lord Shade," a Zellat was saying nervously as he stood over his master. "Lord Shade, are you all right?"

"What?" said Shade, as he slowly gathered his senses and shivered violently, "of course I'm all right. It was just a dream."

Shade looked around fearfully in the darkness.

"Lord Shade," said the Zellat quietly, "one of Gaia's guards is here. She wants to see you."

"Gaia?" said Shade, shivering again and thinking of Abrazo.

"Yes, Lord."

"I've no time to see Gaia. Caius has already taken more Zellats to finish off these usurpers and morning is not far off."

"Yes, Lord," said the Zellat, "but she insists that she needs you."

"Needs me?"

The Zellat nodded.

"Gaia says, she needs me?"

The Zellat was silent.

"Very well then," said Shade, smiling, "if Gaia needs me, I must go to her."

Shade found Gaia standing on her own, near the tree line. Aiko and Rosa were a way off murmuring to each other, and they looked fearfully at him as he arrived. The Zellat guards were standing guiltily around her trying to look as alert as possible.

"Well, my dear?" said Shade sarcastically. "they say you need me."

The old mare smiled.

"Shade," she said quietly, "I am so glad you came."

Shade looked carefully.

"I've been worried," Gaia went on. "I've hardly seen anything of you of late."

"I thought you hated me to be near you," said Shade coldly.

Gaia dropped her eyes.

"I know, I know," she said. "I did in the past, but now…"

"But?"

"I am so lonely, Shade."

A flicker of suspicion crossed Shade's eye, but he felt a tightening in his stomach too. To hear Gaia talk so tenderly was something he had never known before and now his heart was wrestling with his instinct.

"Go on," he said.

"Maybe I've been wrong," whispered Gaia. "Maybe I've misjudged you. I can see now how much you've done for our kind, how everyone else is in fear of us."

Shade stirred. Her words were so strange and unfamiliar, yet so much what he had always longed for, that he felt a sudden yearning in his heart.

"I need to talk to you, Shade," Gaia went on, "as we have never talked before. Then maybe I will understand. I have thought of late that perhaps your cruel… your anger was because of me. Because I didn't love you."

For the first time, Shade's eye looked sad.

"Yes," he said, "Perhaps I have been angry. Perhaps…"

"It must be hard for you," said Gaia, "with so much responsibility for everyone. Even a lord needs friends."

"I do get lonely," said Shade quietly.

"There is so much I want to tell you Shade," said Gaia as passionately as she could.

"Go on, my dear, go on."

"No, Shade, I can't. Not with all your guards about. Tell them to go away, just for a little while. Then we can talk."

Shade hesitated, but his longing had already overcome his natural suspicion. He suddenly swung round to his Zellats.

"You," he cried, "get out of here. All of you. I will come to you when the morning comes."

The startled Zellats thought Shade was angry with them and without a word, they did as they were told.

"Aiko, Rosa, my friends. I want to talk with Shade. Will you leave us for a while?"

Her eyes trained on the mares and there was a hardness and clarity in them. They knew full well what Gaia wanted them to do.

"So, Gaia," said Shade quietly when the mares had left as well, "we're alone at last."

"Yes."

"What would you say to me?" whispered Shade tenderly.

"Only this," cried Gaia suddenly. "I hate you, Shade, and I will always hate you."

Shade looked back at her in amazement.

"In your vanity do you really think," blazed Gaia, "that I could feel anything for you? You who murdered Abrazo and destroyed everything I ever cared for."

"Then why?"

"To get you alone. Aiko and Rosa are already escaping, and now I am going to join them, and I will be free of you forever.

Shade stood shock-still as Gaia backed away into the darkness. He was too startled to do anything at all.

"But first, there is someone I would like you to meet," called Gaia. Then she was gone galloping after her friends.

Shade paused. His senses were tingling. And then he heard it, a twig breaking behind him. He swung round to see a stallion stepping from the trees. It was still dark, but the light was coming now, slowly filtering through the strangely warm air. His eyes opened wide as he looked at this proud face. The likeness with his father struck Shade immediately. His eye sprung open, in the knowledge of who was standing in front of him.

"So," he murmured, "you have come at last?"

"Yes, Shade," answered Star, "I have come."

Shade nodded. He was thinking hard but realised that while the Zellats were so far away, he was desperately vulnerable.

"And you are going to kill me?"

"It is you, Shade, who sends assassins," answered Star coldly.

"Ah, yes," said Shade, "and I should have trained him better. You just won't die will you, Star? Quite the survivor, aren't you? Then let me tell you something. I am pleased to meet you at last."

"Pleased?" said Star.

"Oh, yes," said Shade. "We are not so different you and me."

"We have nothing in common."

"Oh, but we do. We both believe we have a destiny. I just believed that violence was the way to achieve this. The way of man."

Shade was unsettling Star, and he revelled in this.

"You have your mother's eyes," Shade continued. "She's an exceptional mare, Star and intelligent too. When I think of how she just tricked me!"

"Then you knew that she was my mother?"

"I have known for years."

"So, you know about the Prophecy. That I was changed at birth."

"Still the Prophecy," said Shade. "Do you think you can frighten me with all that?"

"Why don't you believe it?" said Star.

"Why?" said Shade angrily, "because it is lies. If you want something, you have to take it. Just like the humans do. If they want something, they just kill and get it! They don't live by some tale or superstition."

"You spread a different kind of lie," said Star.

"No, I bring them power and reason. And with this power, I will give them freedom, and we will control all animals, maybe even mankind."

"You bring only death and violence. But I will show you another way when the Prophecy comes to pass."

"You're a fool Star, fear is the only way to control. This is man's way."

"You forget Shade, I too have knowledge of man. There is good in man."

"You are just a dreamer!" he spat. "Man will never help us, they only take."

"Man has already helped me, Shade, more than once. And there is goodness there."

"Ha!" scoffed Shade.

"What knowledge can there be that is more than mine? All my life I have looked at man, learnt from him, learning from the power that is greater than all animals."

"Is that what you learnt when you were taken in by humans," said Star coldly.

"So you know?" he gasped.

"Yes, Shade. I know."

Shade suddenly felt a terrible weakness enter him.

"I know everything Shade…Everything." Star's eyes fixed on Shade. I know you killed a human foal," he said sadly, his voice echoing into the coming dawn.

Shade's eye peered back. He suddenly felt afraid.

"But I don't know why," whispered Star.

"And you would never understand," said Shade quietly.

"Tell me," said the stallion.

Shade peered back at Star, and there was fury in his look.

"Very well. My father, the great Balan, took control of the Guardians in the north. He discovered the pictures in the cave and saw the violence of man and what they did to our kind when the first horses came to these lands. He realised that by violence, man could control us and all animals. My father set out to take back that control. He too sacrificed our kind to the gods, as did man, thinking that power would be his. Nothing happened. The gods do not exist, and you are a fool to believe anything. My father and I were cast out, and my father died. I vowed on his dead body that I would get revenge. I was taken in by humans, and I studied them. Then, the time came, and the human foal was born."

"And you stole it and killed it. Why?"

"Why?" cried Shade. "Because I wanted to be stronger than them. Stronger even than Arion. Look what they did to us. I told myself that I would never fear anything ever again. I wanted the strength of their spirit to enter me and make me invincible."

Star looked at the burning fury in Shade's eye, and he realised that the story that Athos had told him was true. He had hardly dared believe it.

"So you did…"

"Yes," spat Shade, on the edge of frenzy, "so I ate the heart of the human foal."

Star looked at Shade, and he felt almost sorry for him.

"Then, the madness is in you. You have transgressed the oldest of lore."

"I worship nothing. Your gods cannot harm me." Shade was trembling with rage.

"My secret was safe until you found out. The other horses will never understand, why I did it, why it was necessary. I would have taken my army north and destroyed the Guardians and gained my revenge and buried my secret with them, but you had to get there first."

"You are evil Shade," said Star.

"Grow up Star, the world is evil. If you do not take what you want, then you will die. I am going to take everything."

"You must be destroyed," said Star but there was little anger in his voice.

"And how will you do that," snorted Shade. "I am old, and you could kill me here and now. But there are those who will step into my place, like Caius and others, I have trained. This army I have assembled is invincible, and I will destroy anything that stands before us."

"You're wrong. For other horses are coming."

"Your puny allies can do nothing to me. By tomorrow your friends will be destroyed. They are trapped now at the canyon. If you kill me they will still be destroyed and how will that have served your god? You have failed Star, failed."

"Not yet," said Star, "and that is why I have come to tell you. I thought I might be able to reason with you, but now I see that is impossible, the madness has taken you and eaten your soul. Well, Shade, know this. I will be there tomorrow, and Arion will be with me, and you will be defeated."

Shade looked at the stallion standing there so defiantly, and he suddenly felt a strange admiration for him.

"Then come and fulfil your Prophecy if you dare. For not even you know the ending yet, or your fate."

Star stared back at the old stallion and inside he was also trembling, but he snorted and turned away. The light was cracking all around them now.

"Mark me," he whispered, "tomorrow I will come again. So look out for me, Shade and fear me."

With that, Star was gone.

Shade stood there shaking in the grass.

"Very well," he hissed, "then if I have to, I will fight Arion himself."

Star galloped as swiftly as he could away from that place towards the canyon. He was thinking now of his friends, and of Ella. He would be with them soon, to fight and die if necessary. But first, he had something to do, to find the trapper who had helped him and to get the wood with sap that burnt with human's orange light.

Chapter 19

"We must rush them now, break through the pass," said Tarn gravely.

The sun was high in the canyon, and the clouds had cleared. The light was glittering off the lake as the beleaguered Band faced the day. The night had been hard for all of them, but at least the stand-off gave them some rest bite. All morning they had discussed what to do, and now as the day wore on, the urgency of their situation was crowding in on them again. They had noticed that the Zellats seemed a little distracted and that there were fewer than ever protecting the neck of the pass.

"It shouldn't be impossible to get through," said Armand, "if we stay close together, run fast and drive at the centre, we might get through. We must watch our flanks because the others on the slopes will be sure to hit us from the sides."

"Ella," said Tarn, "I want you and Misty in the centre."

"No," said Ella firmly, "I can kick and-"

"Please, Ella, you've done enough already. Do as I say."

The mare looked steadily back at Tarn, and then she nodded.

"Well then," said Tarn quietly, "Let's get to it."

He turned to the Band. There were now over one hundred and sixty of them. He smiled, proud to lead them. At that moment he felt that their togetherness could defeat anything.

"Come on," he cried suddenly, "let's show these Zellats what we're made of."

Tarn began to run, and Armand and Chub charged after him. Then they were all running, what a sight. Sleek beauties, wild mustangs with muscles that rolled underneath their supple coats, that glinted in the rising morning sun. Majestic frames and flowing manes that unfurled and whipped as the wind caught them. Their hooves pounded the ground in a natural canter, their haunches quivering as they charged forward. Ella tossed her head, and her eyes, full and genuine saw through the danger and trusted her safety and her soul to the great spirits, and for a brief moment, she imagined that she was back on her beloved Prairie with the sun on her back.

"Ella," cried Tarn, as they ran, breaking the spell. He was just in front of her.

"What is it?"

"When you were in the herd, did you hear or see anything of my mother?"

Chub overheard the question, and he looked painfully at Ella.

"Nothing," called Ella sadly.

The Zellats in the pass saw them coming, but many in their number had wondered away to graze, and others were still scattered on the slopes. They hadn't expected their quarry to make a breakout just yet. They began to rally, and their commander bellowed his orders, but when Tarn and his Band hit them, they had, if not quite the element of surprise, then the force of an attack on their side.

Soon the narrow pass was alive with fighting horses, rearing, kicking and biting. Tarn's forces were battling their way through. Other Zellats joined the melee from the slopes, but they were beaten back, as every effort was turned to breaking through the pass.

Ella and Misty stayed in the middle of the pack, and they both wished they could contribute more, but at this moment they were protected on all sides from the fighting. At one point a Zellat managed to push passed, but Misty lashed out with her back hoof, catching him in the face just as he turned his head.

"We're going to make it, Ella," cried Misty amid the throng, "we're going to make it."

Ahead of them, they could already see the mouth of the canyon.

But a wall of Zellats rose up in front of them and again the way was barred.

"One last push," cried the bloodied and exhausted Tarn. "That's it," he encouraged as the way was opened again. But as he uttered those words, his legs buckled under the side assault of two of the enemy, swamped under several kicks and bites. He stumbled and fell, somersaulting over with the ferocity of the attack. Around them, the Zellats were being driven back as they swept through the pass. Ella rushed back to Tarn's side. He lay there motionless on the earth.

"Tarn," cried Ella, "Tarn!"

Tarn didn't move.

"Tarn, quickly, get up, before they're on us again," she urged.

But it wasn't the combined assault that had done the damage, for as Ella looked down on his stricken body, she realised that the fall had broken his neck.

"No, it can't be," she gasped.

But he didn't stir. Chub came to Ella's side and stared down in amazement at his dead friend.

"I didn't even have time to tell him about his mother," whispered Ella bitterly.

"That was one mercy, at least," said Chub quietly.

But there was no time to mourn.

"Quickly," cried Nacho behind them, "they're coming again."

Blind with rage, Ella and Chub began to gallop after Nacho towards the head of the pass, where they could see Armand leading the rest out into the flatlands beyond. Armand had no idea of what had happened, and now his heart was thrilling with courage and pride as he raced away. They had made it through.

But as they cleared the far end of the pass and galloped away, with the forest curving to their left and a river swerving to the right with mountains beyond, they were met with a sight that threw them into confusion and despair. Armand pulled up in horror, and his fighting Band did the same.

There in front of them, as far as the eye could see, were a thousand enemy horses, stretching from the forest to the river, waiting silently in the day.

Ella, Chub and Nacho reached them too, and though their thoughts had been on Tarn, lying dead in the pass, the sight of this wall of terror swept everything else from their minds. They looked at one another in despair.

"We could turn back," cried Blake.

"No, they're coming through the pass," panted Chub.

"Quickly make for the trees," shouted Armand, but as they did so, more Zellats emerged into the daylight at every passable point of the forest.

"The river," cried Chub, but on the far bank, a line of stallions were already moving up to block their escape.

There on the vast plain, the proud hundred and sixty stood, dwarfed by the ranks of the enemy that surrounded them.

"Armand," cried Misty desperately. "Armand, what shall we do?"

"Tarn," said Armand, suddenly walking from the vision of hopelessness, "let's try to…"

But as he looked round Armand realised that Tarn was missing.

"Tarn, where's Tarn?"

He was looking at Ella, and the mare shook her head sadly.

"He never made it through the pass."

Armand gazed back at her in horror, but now his instinct began to rally, and he realised that without Tarn they were leaderless. He turned to scan the land ahead, and almost immediately his eyes settled on a patch of ground to the west, near the forest, that rose to a hillock of rock and heaped earth with a single, large birch tree growing in its middle but wide enough for some horses to mount a defence.

"There," cried Armand, "we'll make our stand there."

Blake had seen it too, and he was already ordering the others towards it. Like a flock of birds, they swung together desperately galloping for the higher ground. The Zellats saw what they were doing, and instantly fifty of them broke from the facing wall of horses and rushed forward to try and cut them off. But the mound was closer to Ella and the others and as Shade's horses drew near, Blake, Armand had already reached it. Ella, Misty, Chub and the others flowed up its sides after them, and as they did so, the Zellats pulled up and headed back to the main army.

There they settled. The four old friends Nacho, Blake and the rest gathered around the tree. They made a brave sight, but a desperate one as well. Silence fell on the Plains, and the Band of friends waited, but the Zellats didn't move. The enemy across the river made no attempt to cross the water, and to the east, the Zellats stayed in the shadows of the trees. Behind them, the pass was sealed again, but they did not advance either. They were all waiting.

Suddenly, the distant ranks of Zellats in front of them began to stir and then parted. Through the middle of them came two horses. From the hill, the friends recognised Caius and at his side was an old stallion.

"Shade," snorted Blake.

Shade and Caius had reached the front of the line, and they began to range up and down the columns of waiting stallions, inspecting and nodding approvingly.

Shade smiled inwardly. His night terrors and the shock of meeting Star had passed away with the morning, and now his courage swelled as he looked on. His enemy were so few compared to his vast army, the odds over ten to one. Shade had some concerns of Star's words that the Guardians and their followers might still come, his scouts had seen nothing at all and he knew that they would never reach here in time. They were doomed.

"He has lost, Caius," whispered Shade delightedly.

Caius nodded. He had been amazed when Shade told him of Star's visit, but any fear that had woken in his heart was dispelled by the sheer might of his massive army.

"Today we will put an end to this… Prophecy," said Shade. "Before nightfall, we will finish this once and for all, and the name of Arion will never again be spoken. And if he dares to come, we will end Star's life too."

Caius smiled.

"I will watch from those trees," said Shade, nodding casually towards a cluster of cottonwood. "Bring some Zellats to guard me. But first I want to talk to these fools."

Caius gave the order as Shade walked forward. The distance to the mound was some fifty tall tree lengths, but the ground dipped slightly, and in the still air, Shade's voice carried clearly to the waiting Band and across the ranks of Zellats too.

"You, who seek to oppose my way," he cried, "I had thought to let you live, for Caius tells me that you fought well in the canyon. But now I see you, I feel nothing but contempt. You will never see another sunrise."

Shade nodded his head and as the small Band stood there trembling, across the grass came the rising sound of thousands of hooves stomping in unison.

A look of hopelessness came to them all as their heads turned to one another, forlornly.

"I'm frightened Ella," whispered Misty as the sound swelled.

Ella smiled sadly at her sister.

"If we're to die," she answered, "then at least we will die together."

Misty lifted her head. Armand and Chub were listening now, and the friends drew near and looked at each other silently. Chub gazed at Misty, sadly, for he had never even told her what he felt for her. But they had all been through so much together, and they knew each other so well, that words now seemed barely necessary.

"You know," said Chub after a while as he turned to Misty, smiling as he looked into her big deep dark eyes. "I always wanted to tell you that-"

"I know…" interrupted Misty as she nestled her head against his.

At that moment a wave of regret washed over him. He would never have the chance to live life with his true love.

Chub then turned to his friends. "I am proud to have known you all."

"I wish Star could have been here," said Armand.

"No," whispered Ella, "it is better that he's not here. What could he do? I'm glad he's not here. At least I know now that he was never a coward. But I wish… I wish… our parting had not been so terrible."

The friends were silent again and the hoof stomping subsided.

They're coming on, whispered Nacho.

Wave after wave of Zellats advanced towards the mound. Not all of them came. Some three hundred. Walking at first, then trotting, cantering and then breaking into a gallop.

"Chub," said Armand lifting his head proudly to his lifelong friend.

"Armand," replied Chub, equally proud.

"If this is the last story, Chub, then let us make certain it is the best."

Chub nodded and drew his breath. The Band had gathered in concentric rings around the birch tree and as the Zellats advanced, Armand, Chub, Blake and Nacho, stepped forward through their ranks, to each side of the stand.

The Zellats drew nearer and now they could see the fiery menace in the eyes of the approaching enemy. The attackers slammed into the hillock like a tidal wave. Even within the ring of defenders Ella and Misty felt the shock of it. All around them, stallions were fighting, teeth bearing, rearing, kicking, lashing out in blind aggression. In a frenzy of thrusting haunches, horses were pushed from side to side by the massive impacts.

The battle raged on, but in the midst of the desperate melee, neither Ella nor Misty could be sure how her friends were faring. Now and then they would catch sight of Chub or Armand, Blake or Nacho, rising to meet their enemy, hooves clashing, rallying everyone or rushing to the aid of another. All around horses were falling, but they could not tell which side they belonged to as the dust whirled and swirled in the tumult. The one thing the mares were sure of, though, was how hopeless their plight was.

Suddenly, through the stifling heat and murk, a Zellat came careering towards Ella.

"Look out," cried Misty and Ella just managed to step aside as he swung round to kick at her.

From left, Nacho abandoned his position and barged the Zellat against the tree. As the winded Zellat's legs buckled, Nacho's hooves crashed down on his face, delivering a fatal blow to the head. Then Nacho himself fell as several Zellats had forced themselves upon him.

"Help him," cried Ella desperately to the surrounding defenders, "help Nacho."

Those Zellats paid for their brazen courage as four stallions turned and pounded and bit them.

Nacho was severely wounded but still steady on his feet. But as Ella turned back she saw her sister, who had been pushed away in the skirmish, lying among the rocks, bleeding from her head and mouth.

"Noooo!" cried Ella, "not you," she sobbed, her front legs buckling before her.

Ella's head came down above her sister, and she saw a fatal bite mark at her throat. Misty's blood was already sinking into the grass.

The mare's eyes were still open, but they were beginning to stare, then they closed.

"No, Misty, no," cried Ella bitterly. "I should never have allowed you to come with us…"

Ella staggered to her feet, and now she could see that around her the fighting had died down. The Zellats were retreating, and through the thronged stallions, who were beginning to regroup on the mound, Armand and Chub were coming towards her.

"We held them," cried a beaming Chub, "we held them, but it was close." Chub stopped. "No!" he cried. "No!"

The three friends stood over Misty's corpse by the birch tree, their heads bowed. Around them, on the mound, the grass was littered with bodies, along with the many Zellats, some forty of their own had fallen. But while that first terrible charge had almost overwhelmed them, across the Plains, Shade's army was virtually unaffected and already another two hundred from his ranks were advancing again.

"It's finished," said Armand, shaking his head. "We'll never survive another attack."

Chub stamped his hoof on the ground furiously.

"Then we'll kill as many Zellats as we can to avenge Misty."

But now Armand drew Chub aside.

"Chub," he whispered, looking back towards Ella, "will you do something for me?"

"Anything, Armand."

"Will you stay with Ella and protect her for as long as you can?"

Chub stared at Armand. They both knew that they would all die in the next assault, Ella too, but Chub nodded.

"Gladly," he said.

The two friends smiled and made their preparations.

Shade nodded approvingly as he watched the final assault on the mound. It had been too easy. The

Zellats came on as Armand and Blake, and the wounded Nacho ran to the front of the line. Once more they were submerged in a sea of fighting. The ring of defenders began to weaken, and the Zellats broke through.

"Get behind me Ella," cried Chub. The mare did as she was told.

"To me," cried Chub, rising up on his haunches and pounding the air with his hooves, "to me."

But there was no one to help him.

"Come on then," he shouted furiously, "you Zellat s-s-scum."

The Zellats paused, momentarily held at bay by the fury in Chub's eyes. But then they charged at him biting, kicking, rearing. Desperately, Chub held them back, but blow after blow found its mark and finally, too weak to resist, his legs gave way and unprotected, he was at the mercy of his enemy.

As Chub turned his head away, his eyes came in line with the eastern forest. His vision had been impaired by the blows and as his head began to swim and he finally lost consciousness, he fancied he saw a strange sight. In the distance through the fighting horses, Chub saw a light glowing through the day and as his eyes closed, he heard a very faint voice.

"The forest, look to the forest."

At the forefront of the battle, Armand had heard the shout too, and suddenly the fighting horses were disengaging, turning in amazement towards the woods. Now, across the ground, came the sound of terrified horses and the Zellats on the edge of the trees were running left and right in confusion and terror. Armand gasped.

The trees and their branches were glowing. A Strange smoke furled up through the canopy and everywhere a bright orange light began to fleck through the woods. A furious crackling sound came to Armand's ears.

Shade and his army watched in wonder as the Zellats nearest the trees fled.

Whatever was happening Armand knew it could not save them, but at least the distraction had temporarily lost the advantage for the attackers.

"Drive them back," cried Armand, "it's our last chance."

As one, instantly they were fighting again, a new hope filling the defender's hearts. The sight of the light and other Zellats fleeing in terror created confusion. The ranks of the enemy wavered, and suddenly all turned and ran from the mound.

"Chub," cried Ella desperately as Armand ran over to her. But Armand was gazing towards the trees. The glow was growing stronger.

"What is it, Armand? What's going on?" panted Nacho.

"I don't know," whispered Armand fearfully.

Now all the horses fell silent as they watched the furious sparks leap from the trees. The bark was unusually dry from the lack of rain and the strange warmth and already the flames were catching and jumping from branch to branch.

The Zellats that had lined the trees had fled back to the main body of the Great Herd. Among the enemy, a frightened whisper went up as they watched the glow eat away the branches. Only from the centre of the trees was there no orange light and now, from the shadows, stepped a single stallion.

In his mouth, he carried a branch. It was glowing too. He had found his man friend who had lit the flame for him. The stallion reared in the air tossing the branch up in a shower of sparks, bringing his hooves crashing down on the fallen branch, extinguishing its flame.

Armand came forward.

"Star," he gasped. "Star has come."

In the heavens, there was a grumble of thunder, for on the edges of the horizon storm clouds were beginning to gather.

All eyes were trained now on Star as he trotted forward, his head held high, moving towards where Shade and Caius were standing.

When he was about four tree lengths away, he reared on his hind legs in a last show of strength and defiance.

Shade's heart tightened.

"Shade," cried Star, his voice like thunder, "I told you I would come. And I am here. I have summoned man and man's light to avenge my father and all who have died under your tyranny.

Now a furious murmur went up among the Zellats, for they had heard his words and some had understood who this stallion was.

"You," cried Star, addressing everyone, as his head scanned slowly across all before him. "You did not believe in me, the Prophecy, or in Arion, now you will pay the price. I am the one you drove away all those moons ago, and now I have come back to fulfil my destiny."

Many of the Zellats looked to each other in wonder. Next to Shade, Caius stirred fretfully.

"It's true," whispered Caius. "It's true."

Shade's eye seared into Caius and then he snorted in disgust and stepped forwards himself. The Zellat guards around him were looking nervously at their master, but Shade pushed angrily past them.

"Star," he shouted scornfully across the Plain, "you cannot frighten me with your human trickery, although I am impressed with how you made man's fire. But I know that the orange light must feed on the trees and can do no harm to us here. As I told you, I too know the mind of man."

Again the stallions looked nervously to the master, for the sight of the fire in the forest and the smell of burning wood had unnerved them. But Shade's confidence and his knowledge of the orange light seemed to reassure them.

Star stamped the ground.

"Yes, Shade, you know something of the mind of man. But you only know his violence. So why don't you tell them what you did? Why don't you tell them that you killed a human foal and ate its heart?"

A huge gasp rang around. All animals new the consequences of this. They looked in horror at their leader. Shade felt a thousand questioning eyes on his back.

"What of it, Star?" he spat. That is the past. And here we stand face to face."

"Very well then Shade," cried Star. "Come and fight me, on your own if you dare. Too many have died today to waste more unnecessary blood."

Shade smiled coldly.

"How can you harm thousands of us?" replied Shade. "No, you had your chance last night, and you should have taken it. But now you are on your own, and you must pay the price for your belief." The air filled with Shade's maddening triumphant laugh.

"Zellats," shouted Shade suddenly, "take him. Take him now. At first, they hesitated, but their fear of Star was eclipsed by the fear of their mad leader.

"Obey me," cried Shade furiously, swinging round.

Eventually, one Zellat tentatively stepped forward, then another and another.

"That's better," said Shade as twenty Zellats ranked before him.

"Now kill him," rasped Shade.

Suddenly, twenty angry stallions were charging at Star. Star reared one last defiant time before turning and galloping towards his friends on the mound. As the Zellats saw him and thought he was fleeing, more joined in the chase.

"He'll never make it," whispered Ella desperately as Star raced towards them.

His friends were transfixed as Star made for their ranks, but as they watched him, they could see the Zellats closing in from different angles. There were thirty of them galloping in from one direction and another ten from his right.

At that moment a loud 'crack' rang out, and a Zellat horse crashed to the ground dead, blood oozing from a fatal neck wound. All the chasing horses stopped instantly, startled and confused. A second 'crack' sound felled another Zellat.

Suddenly, all the pursuing horses scattered in fear racing off to the distance.

Hidden in the trees a French trapper with his smoking rifle, surveyed the incredible scene.

Shade desperately tried to hold his herd together. They were agitated to the point of stampede.

Back at the mound, Armand and the others stood stock still unable to make sense of what was happening but trusting in their friend and belief in the Prophecy.

Then Armand's appearance changed, a fear came to him.

Ella sensed his fear. "What is it, Armand." Then Ella saw a shadow spreading across the grass.

Then they heard it, the furious sounds of screeching and flapping. The sky was turning black with the wings of tens of thousands of shapes moving through the air.

Star looked to the heavens, "Migisi, thank Arion, you are here."

Armand watched in awe. "Ella, it's the Prophecy, it's happening."

He began to recite the verse.

"Then the skies will darken so. All the animals that seek to harm him will unite to smite his foe."

Birds big and small plummeted from the sky, attacking the Great Herd, pecking at their eyes and clawing at their bodies.

The Zellats lashed out in a frantic frenzy of kicking and galloping. All order was lost as horses tried to rid themselves of their winged foe.

Star reached the mound and looked aghast at the scene of devastation. Chub's eyes were closed. He lay on the ground next to Misty. Blood covered the area around them.

"I've come too late," cried Star bitterly.

"Thanks be to Arion that you have come at all," said Armand. "Star, it's good to see you again."

Star looked helplessly at Misty and Chub. Then he scanned across the others.

"Where is Tarn?" he asked.

Ella shook her head.

"I'm sorry," said Star quietly, "but I had to make sure my mother was safe."

"Your mother, Star?" said Ella with surprise. "Bruma is here too?"

"No, Ella, Bruma is dead. She was not my mother."

Armand and Ella gasped.

But suddenly, Star stepped further forward. He was looking keenly at Chub. The stallion twitched, stirred painfully in the grass and opened his eyes.

"Star," he whispered dreamily. "Star, you're here."

"Stay still, Chub," said Star, "there will be time to heal you if there is time at all."

"But Arion is with us now," said Blake. He too was severely wounded.

"The spirits may be with us," said Star gravely, "but my years of wandering in this world have taught me how strange his ways are, for he may still demand the ultimate sacrifice of us all."

The birds were leaving, and Shade and his commanders were desperately trying to rally their army.

Star looked to the horizon as the last of them passed across the fading sun. Hovering above, was Migisi. She let out a loud screech before disappearing into the distance.

"Thank you," whispered Star, "thank you Migisi and all your friends. But now we have need of stronger help than yours. I only hope they all come."

"They?" said Armand.

"Yes, whatever we do, we must stay on this mound, do we understand."

Shade had managed to bring order back to his army and was once more addressing his fighters.

"See," cried Shade, "they were just birds. No match for us. We are invincible. Look to our enemy they can be no more than sixty left."

Shade was working himself into a frenzy.

"But we are an army. Follow me and victory will be ours. I will show you that I am not afraid."

The Zellats watched their lord and though fear was still stirring through their ranks, for years they had been trained to do his bidding, and in the fading light, Shade looked strangely magnificent. He turned and began to move towards the mound. Caius followed. Then a thousand horses stirred moving on with purpose. More crossed the stream and out from the canyon pass too. The sky was full of heavy rain clouds, swollen by days of evaporation in the unearthly heat.

Star turned to his friends. "If this is to be where it ends, then I would not wish to be with anyone else. I am sorry. Forgive me."

Ella stepped forward, "there is nothing to forgive, Star. You have given us our freedom. I would rather live one day this way than a lifetime of tyranny under Shade."

That same sentiment was evident in the eyes of all who stood there.

Nearer came the enemy, and his friends readied themselves for the terrible impact. Ella suddenly cried out. She could hardly believe her eyes.

"Look, over there."

Near the canyon, Ella spotted a familiar face. "It's Athos and his Guardians."

Armand saw another familiar face with him. "I can see Felise and Lita with the Maidens."

With them, around a hundred horses galloped in. Erith had come, the young horse Star had met at the foothills before they'd climbed the mountain.

Though the arrival of these reinforcements lifted their hearts and swelled their ranks, the odds were still stacked heavily against them. Shade's forces closed in for what all expected to be the final battle.

"Athos," cried Star. "I'm glad to see you, my friend."

"I brought all I could, Star. I fear it may not be enough." said the old horse.

Shade's army charged with fury, nostrils flaring. Closer and closer they drew.

"Arion," whispered Star. "Help us now, Arion."

In the sky, the clouds had grown black, and suddenly there was a rumble of thunder. Lightening flecked off the heavens, and it started to rain. But Shade's army was on them. Star had given strict instructions not to be drawn off the mound, and his valiant heroes fought desperately to stay alive. In the centre, Star raised to meet his enemy lashing his hooves to box or kick left and right. Armand was by his side and Athos too. Despite his age, the old horse fought with the spirit of ten stallions as they held the Zellats at bay. But around them, the defenders were beginning to fall, one after another. It was hopeless. On they fought, bravely for the honour of Arion, but their hearts were fired now only by desperation, and as the rain grew heavier it added to their despair. They could see the light of triumph burning in the enemy's eyes.

"Goodbye, Star," called Ella above the melee, as she caught sight of the stallion.

Star's eyes came level with hers, and the look in them was one of defeat. "Has my destiny brought us to this, Ella?" said Star. "I am sorry for everything."

"Don't, Star," cried Ella. "At least we will rest together. Forever."

But suddenly, the fighting horses heard a sound that froze all their hearts.

It rose amongst them, a terrible howling, the voice of an enemy far more terrifying than any wild horse that faced them. Then the real enemy was moving around them, snarling and biting, tearing at Shade's Zellats.

"He's come, at last!" cried Star gravely, but with triumph in his voice. "Stand firm on the mound, and we will be safe," Star shouted to his friends.

Tens of hungry wolves moved through the ranks of Zellats, their shining, silvery fur glistening in the wet. They growled as they came, slavering and biting, but only at Shade's army. Star's Band stood in awe as Goran's pack moved in for the kill. Then Star saw Kara, the mountain lion leaping and slashing. Chaos ensued. Shade's forces fled in panic.

"He commands the animals," cried one Zellat. Arion has come to punish us. To punish Shade for what he has done."

"Lord Shade," cried Caius in the midst of the fray, but as he turned to his lord, Caius gasped. Shade was surrounded. Three wolves were advancing on him, curling back their lips to show their teeth and growling furiously. Shade was trying to back away, but the old stallion had nowhere to run. He too showed his teeth, but now he looked tired and helpless.

"Come then," cried Shade in his madness, "come Arion. For you have hunted me all my life, haven't you?"

The wolves were about to pounce when suddenly Caius came charging straight at them, but as he did so, the wolves leapt at him, all three at once. Caius was lost. He felt death in his throat. Shade escaped.

"Star, dear Star," whispered Ella from the mound as she watched this unearthly sight. "How?"

"The hunter is among us, we must stay here and be perfectly still." he replied.

Shade's army scattered to the wind. Goran had given instructions to spare those who were passive, so soon the Great Herd had either fled or had surrendered.

"You've won, Star," cried, Ella. "Won."

But Star wasn't listening to the mare. He was looking out into the distance. Near the edge of the pass, he saw an old stallion slipping away.

"Star," cried Armand, running up to him, "Shade is escaping."

"I've seen him," said Star.

"I'll bring some horses and we'll get him."

"No, Armand," cried Star. "I must do this alone."

Star began to run as fast as he could through the driving rain towards the canyon entrance. When he reached it, he caught sight of Shade again at the far end, scrabbling up the steep sides. As he came to the centre of the canyon, he pulled up. On the ground in front of him lay Tarn.

"My poor friend," said Star sadly. "I'm sorry I failed you. You never really liked me, I know that, but

I hope you forgave me somehow. Arion," cried Star bitterly, "must we all die?"

Star suddenly lifted his head in anger and galloped on after Shade.

He stopped at the foot of the steep canyon slopes.

"Shade," he cried, his voice echoing around the rock cauldron. "Face me, Shade."

But the stallion didn't answer. He vanished over a ridge. Star began to climb in pursuit. Up he rose, his hooves slipping on the wet scree. He came over the ridge above the canyon, and again the slope reared up above him. Star couldn't see Shade now, but he could see the narrow path he had taken in the wet. He began to thread his way up the steep mountain side.

He rose higher and higher and kept looking up for Shade. Showers of scree and stone skittered onto his head, and the stallion knew that Shade was somewhere above him. Star came to a thin ledge where the steep slope fell away. The slope was crowned by an enormous rock. The drop below was some ten tree lengths while ahead the slope levelled out. Star paused, fearfully, but he could see that Shade had come this way. He was determined to press on and stepped onto the narrow ledge. Suddenly, stones and rocks were showering all around him. Star reared up in terror, and as he did so, he saw Shade above him on the overhang, pushing at the huge rock. It was beginning to sway, to tilt back and forth on the small tor of stones that barely held it in place and had for centuries, kept it from crashing down onto the ledge below.

"Star," cried Shade furiously, "do you think you can destroy me with your tricks? Well then, join your beloved Arion."

Star gasped as the rock lurched and he saw the light of hatred burning in Shade's eye.

But with that, Star heard a strange sound, a hissing through the damp air. He had heard it before, and something shot passed Star's eyes. He stood amazed as Shade's head was suddenly thrust upwards.

A thin, tapering branch of wood was sticking from Shade's neck, and blood was already pouring from his throat. Shade staggered forward towards the edge of the overhang, away from the rock which had settled back on its precarious perch. He looked down at Star and now the hatred in his eye had turned to confusion and defeat. Then Shade fell, his legs flailing in the air, as his body crashed on the ledge next to Star before rolling and plunging down into the valley below.

In an instant, Star swung round, and on the hillside opposite, he saw a young man. Star's nostrils quivered as the scent of the human came to him. His eyes sprung open in recognition. The young brave had become a man. They both stared across the valley at one another and the wind climbed around them as their breath rose to touch the air. The wind itself seemed to be speaking and saying something to them. A moment of happiness filled their hearts with the memories they had shared. Flying Hawk raised his arm to the sky and screamed out an ululating cry before disappearing back over the hill. Star stood transfixed, then, eventually turned his gaze into the canyon, not quite believing that the evil that had tormented his life was finally dead. It was over.

Star looked to the heavens and once more there was hope in his soul. Then the great stallion turned quietly and walked back down the slope to his friends.

*****

As Star came back through the canyon and looked out across the Great Plains, he saw that Shade's Great Herd had been subdued. To the east, the glow of the forest had gone out. The trees spat and sizzled in the downpour.

The wolves were growling angrily in the rain as they faced the frightened Zellats. Kara was the first to approached Star.

"Now that this is over, we will not be friends again. The third time I will look forward to eating you. The Prophecy is yours." With that, the graceful cat bounded away.

As Star threaded through the ranks of horses, a wondering hush fell over everyone. Ella approached him.

"Shade?" asked Ella.

"Gone, dead." said Star.

Star turned to the frightened horses. "Do not fear the wolves. For this night at least, they will not harm you."

His voice rose above the rain as the Zellats looked at him fearfully. But suddenly one of their numbers stepped forward. "Arion," he cried, dipping his head."

"Silence," shouted Star, immediately subduing the stallion with his eyes," for although I come in his name, I am not he. I am like you. Like you all, even you Zellats."

"A Zellat stepped forward. "I will follow you," he said.

"You must follow nothing but your instincts," Star replied, "and the laws of the Spirits."

The skies grumbled again, and the droplets grew harder.

"But now it is finished," cried Star wearily. "The Prophecy is fulfilled. We are free. Never again will Shade's lies infect us. We must live as Mustangs and nothing else, free to roam. And never again must we kill one another or harm other animals."

The Zellats looked wonderingly at Star.

"But what shall we do?" cried one of them, "without a leader? How will the Great Herd survive?"

"This is not our way," cried Star. Go back to your own Bands, fight for the right to start your own futures, live free and find your own ways."

"So we should fight each other?"

"You should challenge each other for the right to be a Band leader, yes. This is our way, this is Arion's will. For all things, we must fight for our own strength and survival, but not to kill or live by fear."

But at this, the wolves began to growl. They were growing restless. Goran stepped up to Star. Other horses pulled back.

"Star," he snarled, his yellow-green eyes full of hunger, "I came when you called, and I have done my bidding. My debt is now repaid."

The formidable wolf drew menacingly closer to the stallion, but Star did not yield a step.

"Yes, Goran, you have done my bidding," he said, "and Arion's too. For that I thank you."

"I do not need your thanks," snarled Goran angrily. "Remember what I told you, Star. I came because of my debt. Never again will wolves help the wild horses. So fear us now, Star. Balance is restored."

Star looked down into the fiery yellow-green eyes and nodded sadly, but he said nothing.

With that Goran growled again, calling to all his kind. One by one the wolves began to peel away, padding silently through the grass, their eyes glinting furiously in the darkness as they passed through the trembling ranks of horses.

"Ella?" said Star quietly when they had gone.

"Yes, Star," said the mare, stepping up beside him.

"We must tend to Chub and the wounded for many have fallen this day."

Chapter 20

A lone Mustang stood on a rocky outcrop that overlooked the Great Plains of northern Wyoming, just as his father had done long, long ago. He was aged now, but his proud face still carried a strength that all recognised.

Star's bloodline coursed strongly in the valley herds, his second foal, Misty, had her own foals and another of his colts had become a fine looking stallion with mates of his own.

The years had passed, and the Prophecy and the memories of struggle against Shade had all but faded into the mists of time.

Ella had come to join him. She moved closer so that he could feel her presence, yet she stayed quiet, allowing him to remain lost in that moment a while longer. She looked fondly into his eyes. There was a bond between them that all drew comfort from and despite the fact that he was no longer their leader, he still carried the respect of all wild horses of the Plains, living out his life as the healer and the horse that many turned to for counsel in times of need.

His face betrayed a sadness. He sighed, turning to his companion.

"I am tired, Ella, I think I have lost my power to heal. I felt it leaving me, those years ago when I could do nothing for Gaia when she grew ill."

Ella was silent. She knew that his mother's death had hurt Star terribly.

"All my life I have wanted to heal things," said Star, "and I have tried. But sometimes I think there is a wound in nature that nothing can heal."

"And it makes you unhappy?" said Ella quietly.

"In the end, Ella, I had to heal myself," answered Star, "and you have helped me do that. I doubted myself so many times. I should have known from the beginning that you gave me the strength I needed."

Ella nestled her head against his, and there was love in her eyes.

"You're with me now," she whispered.

Star went on quietly, "I sometimes think back on everything that happened, and I wonder if it was a dream, the burden of the Prophecy, my denial, the deaths of so many. They probably would have still been alive if it wasn't for me. If I'd found myself sooner."

"If it weren't for you, none of the Mustangs would be free," replied Ella.

"Maybe."

"Star," said Ella quietly. "I have something to tell you."

"What?"

"When spring comes there will be another little addition to our Band."

Star threw up his head, the shackles of his guilt, forgotten in an instant by the happy news.

"What?" he gasped delightedly.

"Yes," Ella nodded. "I can sense him already. What shall we call him, Star? How about Abrazo?"

"Let's go and tell the others," neighed Star enthusiastically.

Stallion and mare galloped off the hillside and down to the valley below.

As they neared a stream, a group of yearlings stood near the storyteller, listening attentively to his tales.

"He was the only one to defend her," he was saying as he strolled back and forth proudly, "then Chub rose up on his back legs and squealed, to me, to me."

"But we've heard that story," cried one of the yearlings. "Oh, you have, have you?" said the stallion, looking down at him and smiling. "Then what would you like to hear about?"

"I want to hear about the last battle."

"Do you?" said Armand.

"You were there, weren't you?" asked one inquisitive foal.

"I was. I still have a limp," showing his scar to them.

"And Star healed it?"

"That's right."

"Chub's got a scar too, he showed it to me, and he told me that if it hadn't been for Star, he would have died," said another.

"Star saved us all. It is because of him that we are free," said Armand.

"Why doesn't Star heal anymore?" questioned a foal.

Armand looked on the young foal, "he's very busy with other matters, that's all," he whispered. "He has many things to consider, and we should respect that. Anyway, it's too late for another story and time you were back with your mothers."

There was a universal sigh of discontent, but all the yearlings understood that arguing would be a fruitless task. They bade their farewells without too much fuss. Armand watched them leave, and he too was happy.

He looked to the sky and was content and remembered the time when all animals came together. Now they ran free and hunted each other and the strange whisperings that had brought their alliance to fulfil a prophecy had long faded. Over time, horses, beavers, wolves, coyote, prairie grouse, bear and all manner of creatures would tell their tales to their young ones, of a time when once all the animals had been able to understand one another.

The wars of man were over, the fighting of white man against white man, north and south had long since passed, and the bluecoats' war against the pecan skinned people was a distant memory.

In another part of the Prairie, a contented mare galloped away leaving her stallion to walk alone.

His eyes steadied to the horizon, face aglow with the last orange rays just before the time for twilight to beckon the stars.

A wind whipped up, and a faint voice carried on the breeze.

"Star, it is time." The startled stallion's ears pricked, raising his head to the sky where he saw the first speck of yellow, glistening in the early evening heavens. This was the great star of Arion which shone like the glowing embers of a dying fire. His lips bore the semblance of a smile, just enough to show that at that moment he was enjoying his thoughts, whatever they were.

Again the wind rose, whipping up the dust into a swirling eddy, "Star, it is time."

The old stallion suddenly felt very weary, and his limbs ached. Star's eyes were misty, and across the darkening red, blue sunset, the billowing purpling clouds rose like mountains before him.

"Arion, is that you?" whispered Star.

The stallion shook his head. "Or is it just a story?" he said to himself sadly, his eyes clouding over and his nostrils swamped by complex scents around him that he could no longer interpret. "And am I just an animal?"

Again the breeze came up, rustling the grass around him and Star stirred once more.

"Whose there?" he whispered looking around him.

"Star…"

"Arion, is that you?"

"Come then," the voice seemed to say.

Star's heart was pounding, and strangely he remembered Flying Hawk. Then visions of all his friends came to him, of Migisi, of Goran, of Bruma and Gaia, of Nanuq and all smiled down on him.

"One more journey, then, before it's all over?"

If only he had the strength. If only he were a young stallion again.

Then suddenly, Star was running, running like the wind with his head held high and proud once more. His mane was flowing and whipping in the breeze as his hooves pounded in a gallop like thunder on the ground, haunches quivering as they rocked forward, nostrils flaring.

The stallion was climbing the sky, lifted up on the high slope of mauve-white, free to run with the Mustangs forever.

On the Prairie, in the wilderness of America, still in the soft, swaying grass, lay the body of a single stallion. Star had passed into eternity.

ABOUT THE AUTHOR

I was born and raised in a small seaside town of Cardigan on the west coast of Wales.

After University, I spent many years working in London before finally moving from the city to the countryside, eventually settling in the idyllic Cotswold region of England, where I've had more time to focus on my writing.

From a very early age I had a keen interest in crafting stories and would get lost for hours in my adventures. My working career in predominantly senior marketing and creative positions enabled me to continue this childhood passion and fuelled my dream to eventually attempt to write a full blown novel.

I found books by authors such as Richard Adams and William Horwood fascinating, where they used animal subject matter to deliver human stories and this genre very much inspired me in the direction I would take for my first novel, *A Squirrel's Tale* and subsequently with the *The Prairie Drifter* series. "Journey of Discovery", and "The Long Road Home."

My biggest hope is that people really enjoy the characters and the journey they take as much as I enjoyed creating them.

Connect with Richard

I really appreciate you reading my books and hope you have enjoyed the concluding part of The Prairie Drifter series. If you have not read the first book, The Prairie Drifter, Journey of Discovery, you can purchase it via Amazon in paperback and Kindle. All my books are available at all good bookstores and other ebook formats. For more up to date information about me please go to my social media page and friend me on facebook.

Friend me on Facebook:
www.facebook.com/Richard-Wyn-Jones-1459055444359894/

Follow me on Twitter: http://twitter.com/richardjonesgbr

<u>**Other Books:**</u>

<u>A SQUIRREL'S TALE</u>
ISBN: 9780993067402
Available through all major bookstores and all online providers in paperback and all ebook formats and for worldwide distribution via Amazon.co.uk & Amazon.com.

<u>THE PRAIRIE DRIFTER – Book 1 – Journey of Discovery</u>
ISBN: 9780993067426
Available through all major bookstores and all online providers in paperback and all ebook formats and for worldwide distribution via Amazon.co.uk & Amazon.com.